"Don't I get to kiss you good night?"

Reyn's words made Caitlin's pulse beat erratically, but she forced her expression to remain unchanged as she coolly tilted her head to one side.

Reyn turned her to face him. "Good-night kisses on the cheek are for sisters, and you're not that—are you?" He leaned down to brush her lips with his.

It was meant to be a light touch, a teasing caress. But Caitlin's lips clung instinctively to his.

She drew away, catching the flash of surprise in Reyn's eyes, and she smiled with hard-won composure. "Good night, Reyn."

Reyn stared at her, his eyes narrowing. "Good night, Caitlin."

Their kiss had started—and ended—innocently enough, but it awakened a spark of desire that was anything but innocent.

D0036384

Samantha Day, a Canadian author, started
work on her first novel—a futuristic story,
complete with romantic hero and heroine—when
she was fourteen years old. Having long perfected
the art of daydreaming, she now shares her
fantasies with a devoted readership and makes
romance writing her full-time occupation.

Books by Samantha Day

HARLEQUIN ROMANCE
2672—THE TURN OF THE TIDE
2840—FOR KARIN'S SAKE
2923—THERE MUST BE LOVE
3015—UNDER A SUMMER SUN

A LOVE
TO LAST
Samantha Day

Harlequin Books

TORONTO • NEW YORK • LONDON
AMSTERDAM • PARIS • SYDNEY • HAMBURG
STOCKHOLM • ATHENS • TOKYO • MILAN

ISBN 0-373-03127-0

Harlequin Romance first edition June 1991

A LOVE TO LAST

CHAPTER ONE

"YOU LOOK AWFUL," Gabrielle stated bluntly, taking in Caitlin's pale face and the dark circles under her eyes.

"Thanks a lot," Caitlin Carr said, her response sounding more tired than sarcastic. She tucked an afghan around her feet and rested her head against the back of the couch.

"Everything *is* okay, isn't it?" Gabrielle asked, her worry reflected in her voice.

Caitlin nodded. "It was just a routine appendectomy, no complications, nothing out of the ordinary." Her reassuring smile did little to chase the weariness from her face. "I'm just a little rundown, I guess."

"That's an understatement. I told you last spring you should take the summer off instead of loading yourself down with courses."

Caitlin's smile deepened. Gabrielle was being protective again. Usually it annoyed her when people thought that because of her youthful appearance and tiny frame, she needed looking after. But with Gabby it seemed right and natural, because she treated everyone in the same caring manner.

"I had no choice," Caitlin said mildly. "Not if I want to finish my degree this year."

"Fat lot of good a master of education will do you if you're too exhausted to teach. Those kids of yours take a lot out of you."

Thinking of her class of needy children, Caitlin sighed. "But they're worth it. How are they coping, anyway?"

"Not bad, considering. There were a couple of blowups, but Neil seemed to handle himself okay—he might not have a lot of experience, but he's got the right touch. The kids are responding to him. Which reminds me—" Gabrielle opened her purse and pulled out some folded papers "—he gave me some get-well pictures they drew for you."

With a smile of anticipation, Caitlin took the pictures and looked through them. They were as varied as the kids she taught, ranging from Peter's carefully controlled drawing and precise lettering to Riley's scribbled crayoning. The fact that Neil had actually managed to get Riley to do anything was a lot in itself.

The pictures made her feel better. They confirmed that Neil had taken control of the classroom and was able to work with the children. She'd worried that the substitute teacher called in after her emergency operation would do little more than baby-sit while she was gone. Her classroom was never easy to handle and a change in routine would result in chaos. The kids were already so far behind, both academically and socially, that every delay made their eventual integration into regular classes that much harder.

She looked up from the drawings with a smile. "Tell Neil thanks, Gabby."

"I will. Does that mean that you'll be able to relax and enjoy the rest of your sick leave?"

Caitlin grimaced. "I don't know—five weeks is a long time. I've got nothing to do but review what I've already studied. I finished writing the last of my papers a month ago."

"So why don't you take a real break? Go visit your mother or something."

Caitlin shook her head quickly. "She's got a new boyfriend—I'd only be in the way." *And I've had enough of that,* she added to herself.

Gabrielle's dark eyes looked thoughtful as she reached for her coffee mug and took a sip. "You can be alone, right?" she asked suddenly. "I mean, you don't need to have someone with you in case something goes wrong or anything?"

Caitlin looked at her curiously. "No—like I said, I'm perfectly fine. Why?"

"Well, I've told you about my brother—my stepbrother—Reyn?"

Caitlin smiled. "In detail." Although she'd known Gabrielle only a few months, she knew all about the Picard family. Gabby was a perfect nickname.

Gabrielle grinned, dimples flashing. "I guess I *have* mentioned him once or twice. Anyway, he's got this cabin near his house—I asked you to come with me this summer, remember, but you were busy with your courses. Why don't you go stay there, get away for a while?"

"Thanks, Gabby," Caitlin said, shaking her head, "But I don't think so."

"Reyn won't mind, if that's what you're thinking. The place is there for me and my sister to use whenever we want. It's nothing fancy,'' she went on, "but there is indoor plumbing, and it's just back of a cliff overlooking the ocean. It's a really pretty place, Cait— and when's the last time you got out of Vancouver? Just think, you could relax in front of a fire after walking along the beach collecting driftwood..." Her voice trailed off and she grinned at the look on Caitlin's face. "You want it—go for it."

"It does sound tempting," Caitlin admitted. "But the place belongs to your brother. I'd like to know what he has to say about this."

Gabrielle shrugged. "Like I said, it's there for us to use. It's not even in sight of the main house, so you don't have to worry about interrupting his painting or anything. But I'll phone him if you want me to. That is, if you're interested."

"I might be. Talk it over with Reyn—if he doesn't mind someone being there, I'll consider it."

"Great!" Gabrielle smiled widely. "I think it's just what you need." She glanced at her watch. "I gotta run. I told Yvan I'd meet him at seven." She pulled on her jacket and zipped it up. "I'll phone Reyn tonight," she said as she opened the door to leave. "Talk to you tomorrow," she added with a little wave, then shut the door behind her.

Caitlin settled back on the couch, thinking about Gabrielle's offer. She would enjoy getting away from the city for a while. It had been a long time since she had walked quiet beaches and breathed air untainted by car exhaust. The idea held a lot of appeal.

Would Gabby's brother go along with it? Reyn Picard, renowned wildlife artist, undoubtedly valued his privacy and might well veto his sister's suggestion.

If he did, she could still consider renting a place for a few days. But it would be expensive, even in the off-season, and money was something Caitlin handled carefully. She couldn't afford to pay the rent on her apartment *and* a cottage and still manage to send her mother the usual monthly check. Unless she dipped into her savings—and that was something she was loath to do. No, if Gabby's brother was opposed to the idea she would stay where she was.

Caitlin looked around her living room. She had lived in her smallish two-room apartment ever since she'd started teaching, five years before. The streets below were filled with the hustle and bustle of inner-city life, but her apartment was relatively cheap and quite comfortable.

An alcove overlooking the busy street made the living room seem larger than it was. Almond paint warmed the walls and provided contrast to large oak-framed windows. A colorful area rug lay on the gleaming wood floor in front of an overstuffed couch piled with bright cushions. Leafy plants gave the room an airy look and a Japanese screen hid most of the tiny kitchen and eating area. Carefully chosen prints of West Coast Indian art decorated the walls. It might not be a lot by some standards, but it was all hers. It was home.

Caitlin got up to take the coffee mugs to the kitchen. She placed them in the sink, then absently rubbed her side. The stitches were gone and the incision was healing nicely, according to the doctor, but it was still tender, a reminder that she wasn't ready to go back into the classroom.

Gabby was right. She didn't look much better than she felt. Dark circles underscored eyes that were normally a clear ice-blue. Now they lacked luster, looked washed out. The shine was gone from her dark auburn-hued hair, which was badly in need of a cut. Her skin, usually pale and creamy, seemed ashen. She looked delicate and fragile, more waiflike than ever.

Caitlin knew that her rundown condition was caused by more than the operation. She'd been pushing herself too hard. How many evenings and weekends—how many summers—had been devoted to study? And her job was demanding, physically exhausting at times, always emotionally draining. Always there was the knowledge that in spite of her efforts and caring, not all of the children could be helped. Some were doomed to drift through life on the periphery, unable to overcome the chaos of their upbringing. That was what kept her at her studies, the hope that a little more training might give her the means to help one more child.

But she wasn't going to help anybody if she was too worn-out to teach. Rather than fret about her enforced time off, she should look upon it as a chance to relax, indulge herself. It would be a first.

I'll start by making a good meal for myself, she thought, aware that she needed to replace the weight she'd lost since the operation. Slight to begin with, she was now alarmingly thin. She opened the fridge and peered in, but found nothing there that tempted her. Finally she heated some soup and sipped it slowly. But it wasn't long before she pushed the bowl aside with a look of distaste. She got up and went to her bedroom. Climbing into bed, she pulled the comforter over herself and fell into an exhausted sleep. Lately, sleeping seemed about the only thing she was able to do easily.

"THERE'S NO PROBLEM. Really." Gabrielle continued her reassurances as she loaded a suitcase and a box of groceries into Caitlin's old car. She slammed the trunk shut, then dug in the pocket of her jeans for a key. "Here," she said, handing it to Caitlin. "Go and enjoy yourself. Relax. Eat. Fatten up—or at least fill out a bit. You look like a twelve-year-old."

Caitlin made a face. "Thanks a lot," she said as she took the key and put it into her purse. "And you're *sure* your brother doesn't mind?"

"How many times do I have to tell you? Everything's been taken care of. Now get going. You'll miss the ferry if you don't hurry." Unexpectedly she gave Caitlin a hug. "Look after yourself."

"Thanks, Gabby." Caitlin hugged her back. It felt good to know someone cared. She got into the car and started the engine. "Don't forget to water my plants."

"I won't," Gabrielle promised. "Drive carefully now," she added, waving as the car pulled away.

Caitlin waved back, then turned her attention to the road. Morning rush hour was just beginning to thin out, but traffic was still slow, hindered by a steady fall of rain. As Caitlin headed toward the ferry at Horseshoe Bay, she hoped the weather would clear. Maybe some nice sunny weather would make her feel brighter, cheerier. Right now she felt as dull as the day.

The ferry ride to Nanaimo was uneventful. Caitlin nursed a mug of tea, staring through the rain-misted windows, seeing nothing but low gray clouds touching rolling gray waters. She shivered and looked away, taking a sip of tea, wondering if she was doing the right thing. She felt cold and tired and there was still another hour and a half of driving ahead of her, as well as another ferry ride—a shorter one admittedly, but still time-consuming. And all she wanted to do right now was crawl into her own bed in the warmth of her own little apartment and sleep.

She was exhausted by the time she finally reached the tiny island off the east coast of Vancouver Island, and it took another half hour before she found Reyn Picard's cabin. After she parked her car in the driveway, she sat for a few moments looking around.

The setting was nice. Even with the steadily falling rain, she could see the beauty of the place. Towering cedar and hemlock trees bordered the clearing, thick green branches giving subtle contrast to rain-streaked bark.

The cabin was not nearly as impressive as its surroundings.

It looked dark and unwelcoming. Cold. Dank. Caitlin shivered and, with a tired sigh, got out of the car. The sooner she went inside and started a fire, the sooner she could relax.

The porch leading to the front door was slick with rain. Green moss rimmed the steps. Water sluiced down from the cedar shake roof, wetting her. Caitlin fitted the key into the lock, turned it and pushed the door open. The inside was dark and smelled damp. She fumbled for a light switch, found one and flicked it on. To her relief, the electricity worked.

There was one large room with a tiny bathroom off to the side. Bunk beds lined the walls. A lumpy old couch and equally aged-looking chairs crowded around a Franklin stove. There was an old electric range in one corner, and an even older fridge opposite. In between was a counter covered with worn gray arborite. Caitlin shivered in dismay. It was far rougher than she had anticipated. Even the floor hadn't been finished. It was just sheets of plywood with a couple of shabby scatter rugs.

No doubt it was perfectly adequate when Gabby came there with friends and family during the summer. Then, most of the time would be spent on the beach. But during a mid-November rainstorm it was dank and gloomy. Caitlin felt like turning around and heading for home.

But it was late and she was exhausted. She was committed for one night, anyway. *I'll get a fire going in the wood stove,* she thought, *then unpack what I need for tonight. Maybe it won't seem so bad then.*

There was enough dry wood inside to get the fire started but not enough to keep it going all night. As there was no other source of heat, Caitlin made several trips to the woodpile behind the cabin. She hoped the wood would dry out by the time she needed it.

After bringing in her suitcase and the groceries, she sat, worn-out, by the fire. The room still felt damp and she was chilled right through. Finally she got up, found a battered aluminum pot and heated some soup. She felt warmer when she'd finished eating, but her spirits remained low. To add to her depressed gloomy mood, she felt a cold coming on. She started sneezing and her eyes were swollen and watery.

Just what I need, she thought as she picked up her sleeping bag. She unrolled it on the lumpy couch, wanting to be near the warmth of the fire. She threw on some more logs, which hissed damply as the flames licked them. Then she turned out the light and crawled into the nylon-covered bag.

Except for the flickering of flames and the popping of wood as it heated and began to burn, the room was dark and quiet. Very quiet. Used to the constant hum of traffic, the distant wail of sirens and the buzz of people coming and going in her apartment building, Caitlin found the silence unnerving. She listened carefully for some sound from outside, but heard only the wind moaning through the trees and brushing branches against the cabin walls.

Tears of exhaustion slipped down her cheeks, and she wished she'd had a real home to return to after her surgery. A warm home with loving parents who cared about what happened to her, who would pamper and spoil her while she recovered.

It was a useless self-indulgent dream. Angry with herself, Caitlin wiped the tears from her face. She'd be okay. She could take care of herself. She always had.

Twisting around on the couch, she pulled her legs up and hugged her knees to her chest, feeling just fractionally warmer. If her mother had been between boyfriends, she might have considered going to stay with her for a few days. But Caitlin knew from long experience that when there was a new man in her mother's life, everything else placed a distant second. Even her daughter.

Caitlin sighed as she stared into the fire. Her parents had been barely seventeen when they married. Caitlin was born five months later. The pressures of assuming adult responsibilities, combined with no help whatsoever from their unsympathetic and distant families, had been too much for the young couple. By the time Caitlin was three, her parents had gone their separate ways, each with bitter memories. Caitlin stayed with her mother. Her father hadn't bothered to keep in touch.

Caitlin and her mother had drifted from one small town in the interior of British Columbia to another. Janet Carr took what jobs she could find between stints on unemployment insurance or welfare. When she worked, it was as a waitress, usually in the local bar. Money was always scarce. Men weren't. Petite and pretty, with an air of helplessness about her, Janet attracted men easily. Most she just dated for a while. A few had moved in.

When that happened, Caitlin would be relegated to the background. When a new man entered Janet Carr's life, for a time she would be bright and happy, in love and on a real high. But reality would gradually set in, dulling the romance. Once the initial spark was gone, she'd become nagging and resentful. Then the fighting would start and before much longer it would be just Caitlin and her mother again. For a while there would be peace in Caitlin's life.

Unable to sleep while the memories paced relentlessly through her mind, Caitlin unzipped her sleeping bag and crawled out to refuel the fire. Shivering, she poked at the logs until the flames finally caught, then, rubbing her hands together, went to make some cocoa.

She huddled on the couch, cradling the mug in her hands. She'd taken enough psychology courses in recent years to realize that her mother was still caught in adolescence, trying to recapture the years she'd lost due to an unwanted pregnancy and early marriage. Most women would have grown with the experience. Janet hadn't.

Caitlin finished her drink and put the mug on the floor. She slid down into her sleeping bag again and pulled it up around her chin, staring at the glow of the fire flickering behind the grate of the stove. Gradually her eyes closed and she drifted into sleep.

SHE WAS SLOW TO WAKE UP the next morning. When at last her eyes flickered open, she could see that the rain hadn't let up. If anything, it was coming down harder and the cabin seemed even damper. The fire had gone out during the night. Reluctant to face the day, Caitlin huddled deeper into the warmth of her sleeping bag. She felt feverish, her head ached and her throat was sore. More than anything, she wanted to be home.

Finally she got up from the couch, reaching immediately for her jacket and slipping it on quickly. There was enough wood and kindling left to start a fire, but more would have to be brought in. Resisting the urge simply to crawl back into her sleeping bag, she opened the door and stepped outside.

The weather had definitely worsened overnight. The rain no longer fell in gentle misty streaks, but was driven by gusty winds.

Caitlin hurried to the woodpile. She would have to make several trips in order not to put too much strain on her incision. The doctor had been very vocal about the perils of too much lifting.

She pushed aside the top layer of wood hoping to find drier pieces underneath. A slow ache was beginning to make itself felt in her muscles, and the cold rain pelted across her fevered face painfully. Grabbing a couple of the drier logs, she turned to go back.

A dog stood between her and the cottage, a wolfish dog with a thick dark ruff and a white face. Half-crouched, ears pricked forward, it watched her closely through strange pale blue eyes.

Gasping in fright, Caitlin dropped her load of wood and backed away slowly. All dogs made her nervous and this one terrified her. It looked feral, ready to attack. As it took a stealthy step forward, she cringed against the woodpile.

"Relax—he won't hurt you."

Caitlin whirled around. A man stood under the trees, his dark eyes flashing with obvious impatience.

He turned to the dog and snapped his fingers. "Come here, Rex. You're scaring the lady." The dog ran to him, haunches lowered as it wagged its tail. A pink tongue came out to swipe at the man's hand. Then the dog sat and stared at Caitlin again.

She straightened warily, relaxing her grip on the piece of wood she'd clutched in a defensive reaction to her fear of the dog.

"I assume you're Gabby's friend," the man said finally, "although you look like you could just as easily be one of her students. I got home this morning to find some garbled message from her on my answering machine. Do you really plan on staying here?"

"For a day or two," Caitlin answered stiffly, irritated by his manner. "If it's okay with you, that is.

Gabrielle assured me it was. However, if it's too much bother, I'll leave."

"I really don't care one way or the other."

Caitlin raised her chin defiantly. "Then I'll stay." She wanted to tell him what he could do with his miserable cottage, but common sense came to the fore. Yesterday's trip had been arduous, and today she felt worse. She'd have to stay until she was somewhat better.

He gave an abrupt nod. "In that case, I'd better give you a hand bringing in some wood."

"I can manage myself, Mr. Picard," Caitlin said firmly.

He eyed her sardonically. "You don't look like you could manage to get *yourself* inside, never mind a few armloads of wood. And you're going to need a lot. This place wasn't built for winter use—you'll be lucky to get it anywhere near warm enough."

Her annoyance built. It didn't help to know that, for once, she felt about as fragile as she looked. "I said I could manage. Please—feel free to go home."

"And let Gabby find out I didn't help her little friend? No way." He began stacking wood into the crook of his arm, then turned to her. "What's your name?"

"Caitlin Carr," she answered, picking up some wood of her own to carry into the cabin. She wasn't going to let him see how weak and tired she really was.

He gave an abrupt nod, added another log to the pile he was carrying, then straightened. He watched, frowning, as Caitlin warily skirted the dog, whose head swiveled as she moved. "I told you he won't hurt you."

Caitlin glared at Reyn. "I don't like dogs."

"You mean you're afraid of them."

She scowled tiredly. "I mean I don't like dogs." She saw the disbelief in his eyes as he edged his way around her to take his load inside. She followed slowly, her eyes lingering as she saw him take the stairs with lithe ease. *It's too bad his manners don't match his looks,* she thought sourly.

He was much as Gabby described—not too tall, and lean rather than broad. Rain had deepened the waves in his dark hair until it almost curled, and even his arrogance couldn't hide the soft velvety darkness of his eyes.

If he had greeted her with a semblance of warmth and welcome, Caitlin realized she might have found herself attracted to him. As it was, she found his presence intrusive. She'd rather be alone than put up with his impatient arrogance. Steeling herself, she went inside.

Reyn said nothing as he brushed past her on his way out for another armful of wood. Caitlin made a face at his retreating back, then dumped her wood into the box by the stove. Why couldn't he have stayed away?

She glanced around once more at the dismal cabin and sighed, feeling the unrelenting ache in her bones deepen. Rubbing her hands together, she held them over the stove, wondering if she'd ever feel warm again. After a moment, she turned and trudged back outside. She hugged her arms to her chest, her body feverish and shivering.

Reyn looked at her closely as she bent to pick up more wood. Her eyes, rimmed by lashes spiked with rain, were huge in her pale face. Dark rain-soaked hair was plastered against her head.

"You look like you're ready to pass out," he said brusquely. "Get inside and dry yourself off. I'll bring in the wood."

"I'm fine," Caitlin said, resenting his tone of command. Quickly she gathered up an armful of wood and returned to the cabin, ignoring Reyn, although she was very aware that he was studying her with annoyance.

This time she stayed inside. Uncomfortable as the cottage was, it was a definite improvement over the conditions outside. She picked up a towel and wiped the water from her face and hair, watching quietly as Reyn dumped another load in the wood box. After glancing at her, he went out again.

Caitlin was tempted to follow just to show him that she could take care of herself, but reason won out. She could feel a tug in her side and shivers rippled through her body. She was exhausted. It would be crazy to push herself further simply to show Reyn she could manage.

She wondered just what message Gabby had left on Reyn's answering machine. Knowing Gabby, she'd probably told him to keep an eye on her. Darn it, she should have anticipated that. While Caitlin might be able to tolerate Gabby's protectiveness, it wasn't something she wanted transferred to Reyn.

She'd hate it if he felt obligated to take care of her out of some sense of duty to his stepsister.

Once he'd brought in the wood maybe he'd return to his own place. In a day or two, when she was feeling better, she would head back to Vancouver and leave him to his peace and quiet.

After dumping one last armful of wood into the box, Reyn stood in the center of the room, brushing off his hands. "That should see you for a few days," he told her.

"Thank you," Caitlin said, managing a stiff smile. He was looking at her closely again with those soft brown eyes, making her feel uneasy.

"Are you all right?" he asked suddenly. "You look washed out."

"I'm perfectly fine, thank you." She saw the disbelief on his face and added quickly, "I'm just a little tired. I didn't sleep well last night."

"I'm not surprised." He looked around with an expression of distaste. "I hope you're not planning to stay long. You don't look like you're up to it."

Caitlin scowled at him. "I told you—I'm fine."

"Good." Reyn pushed up the sleeve of his jacket to glance at his watch. "Damn, I've got to get going." He stopped at the door and glanced back at her. "Look— if you do need anything..."

I'll be sure not to ask you, Caitlin finished silently. She didn't want his help any more than he wanted to give it. "I won't," she said determinedly.

She could tell that suited him just fine. He nodded his head once, then left, shutting the door behind him.

Caitlin sagged with relief, glad he was finally gone. She wondered if she would have been able to hold on to her poise much longer.

She felt awful—shaky and sick, and chilled to the bone. After feeding the fire, she hugged her arms to her chest and huddled close to the stove's warmth, trying to get warm.

Deciding a hot shower would help, she stuffed as much wood as she could into the fire box, then, stripping off her damp clothes, went into the tiny bathroom.

Instead of the hot spray she'd expected, lukewarm water sluiced over her body leaving her thoroughly chilled. *It figures,* she thought miserably, getting out as quickly as she could. She dried off briskly and dressed in a warm fleecy sweat suit. Nothing had gone right since she'd arrived.

Sneezing several times in rapid succession, she left the bathroom, checked the fire once again and crawled into her sleeping bag. The shivers slowly stopped racking her body and she drifted into a troubled sleep.

SHE WAS AWAKENED by a sharp knock on the door. Still dazed with sleep, she lay blinking in the darkened room. Another knock wakened her fully. As she started to sit up, the door opened.

Reyn stood in the doorway. "Did I wake you?"

"It's all right," Caitlin said hoarsely. Her throat was sore and her face was flushed with fever. She rested her head against the corner of the couch wishing he hadn't returned. This time she couldn't possibly pretend she was all right.

He shut the door behind him as he came into the room, then stood frowning as he looked down on her. "You're sick."

"It's just a cold." She watched him warily, hoping he'd go away. Instead, he sat in one of the threadbare armchairs opposite the couch.

"I talked to Gabby," he said. "She shouldn't have sent you here. This is no place to recuperate, especially not at this time of year."

Caitlin nodded tiredly. "I can see that. And I don't plan on staying. I'll leave tomorrow." *If I have to drag myself out of here,* she added to herself.

"Fine—but in the meantime, you're coming home with me."

Caitlin's eyes opened wide. She shook her head quickly, "Oh, no. I'm fine here for another night. Really."

"I insist," Reyn said firmly. "I can't leave you here—it's damp and uncomfortable, and you're obviously not well. And Gabby made me promise."

The mother hen strikes again, Caitlin thought. Surely Reyn could see past her small size and youthful appearance to realize she was old enough to look after herself.

"I don't care what you promised your sister. I'm all right. I can take care of myself."

"Can you? You didn't even have the sense to turn around and go home after you got a look at this place."

"I had every intention of leaving today. I didn't plan on waking up with a cold." She managed to glare resentfully at him. "Goodbye, Mr. Picard. I'll leave tomorrow morning."

Dark, well-defined eyebrows rose sharply. "I doubt that—Ms. Carr. You look flushed and feverish, and you sound like a frog in a spring rain. Do you honestly think you're going to feel up to driving back to Vancouver tomorrow?"

"Yes."

"Come on, be honest now."

Her head dropped back on the pillow. She didn't even have the strength to fight him in spite of her determination. Even if she felt only half as bad tomorrow, she knew she'd find the trip home impossibly arduous.

He leaned forward, resting his arms on his knees. "Do you really want to stay here a moment longer than you have to?"

Caitlin glanced around the damp dark room, then looked at Reyn. "No." The word was scarcely more than a croak. She cleared her throat, swallowed painfully and tried again. "No, not really. But I won't feel comfortable imposing on you, either, Mr. Picard. Thank you, but I can take care of myself."

"Don't be childish. You're obviously sick, and I'm not about to leave you here alone—Gabby'd never let me hear the end of it. Either you come up to my place, or I move in here to keep an eye on you. Neither of us might like it, but that's the way it's going to be. Take your choice."

Caitlin scowled at him, then slid further down on the couch and pulled the sleeping bag up around her neck. Laying an arm over her eyes, she turned her head away from him. Maybe if she couldn't see him, he'd disappear.

"I mean it, Caitlin," he said. The words were spoken softly, but were underlined with determination. "I'm not going to go back and let Gabby know you're still down here—she'll hound me until she knows you're okay. I don't need the interruption."

Reluctantly Caitlin turned to look at him again. A glance at his stern face told her he meant it. Thanks to

Gabrielle, she'd been assigned a guardian, like it or not.

He was growing impatient. "Well?"

Caitlin sighed and pushed herself to a sitting position again. "All right."

"My place?"

She nodded. She might as well be comfortable. It would only be for a day or two, anyway. Just as soon as she could, she'd be on her way back to Vancouver.

REYN STOWED HER BELONGINGS in her car, bundled her into the passenger seat, and drove the quarter mile to his house.

Caitlin felt resigned, too sick to really protest. And in spite of his somewhat overbearing attitude, she couldn't deny that it was a relief to know she wouldn't have to fight her illness alone in that dank little cabin.

She glanced at Reyn as he drove along a narrow gravel road that wound upward through thick stands of tall trees. Even though she hadn't met him before, he wasn't exactly a stranger to her. Gabby had told her all about him. That thought gave her a feeling of satisfaction, as though she had the edge on him. She glanced at him again, her smile disappearing. She might need that edge. He was a difficult man, albeit an attractive one.

"Almost there," Reyn said, turning off onto an even narrower road.

As the view opened up, Caitlin could see his house. It was built of weathered cedar with a high-peaked roof, and rose from the rock to blend with the trees around it. Long windows faced east, overlooking the mainland in the rain-misted distance. A hundred yards beyond the house the land dropped sharply to the ocean far below. It seemed the ideal setting for a wildlife artist.

Reyn parked Caitlin's car next to his own. "You get inside the house," he said. "I'll bring your things."

Her strength to argue long gone, Caitlin got out of the car, shivering as the wind dashed cold rain against her heated skin. She hurried up the stairs to the deck and pushed open the sliding glass door.

The dog stood just on the other side, watching her warily. As it took a step forward, Caitlin quickly backed out and slid the door shut. Huddling in her jacket, she waited for Reyn.

He came up, carrying her suitcase, frowning as he saw her standing in the rain. "I thought I told you to go inside."

"I, uh… It's the dog," she said, hating her fear, yet unable to control it.

Reyn shot her a look of impatience. "I told you, he won't hurt you." He opened the door and ushered her in.

Tail wagging, the dog came to greet his master. Caitlin held back.

"Hi, Rex," Reyn said, rubbing the dog's ears fondly. He glanced at Caitlin, frowning at the look he caught on her face. "You really are afraid of dogs, aren't you? What was it? A bad experience as a child?"

Caitlin nodded, thinking back to one of her mother's boyfriends. Uncle Alec, she'd been told to call him. He had moved in for a few months when Caitlin was seven or eight, bringing his dog, a big German shepherd, with him. It was a well-trained guard dog, and when Caitlin's mother was out of the house Alec would amuse himself by making the dog guard Caitlin. On command, the dog would position itself close to her. Ears pricked and eyes alert, it would growl deep in its throat at her slightest move. The fear roused by both the man and the dog lingered as she grew up.

"I'm sorry," she said, annoyed with herself. "I know it's silly, but . . ."

"Give me your hand," Reyn ordered, reaching out with his own. "It'll help if you let Rex sniff it. Believe it or not, he's just as afraid as you are. He's had a few bad experiences himself."

She didn't want to. As she hesitated, she saw Reyn's finely cut lips curve sharply with amusement. She quickly held out her hand. His cool strong fingers curled around hers as he brought her closer to the dog. She suppressed a shiver that had as much to do with Reyn's touch as it did with the dog. He kept her hand in his, guiding it to softly stroke the fur between the dog's ears.

The feel of her hand in Reyn's was distracting. She hardly noticed the dog. Even its tentative lick didn't really bother her, although she grimaced and croaked, "Yuck."

"Well," Reyn said, his dark eyes lighting with unexpected laughter, "it's a start, anyway." He didn't release her, but rubbed his thumb across her wrist. An odd sensation shot through her and she shivered.

"You're quite feverish." He frowned, and pushing the hair back from her forehead, he laid his palm against her brow.

Made doubly uncomfortable by the scrutiny of his deep brown eyes and his cool touch, Caitlin pulled back, shaking her head. "Please don't," she murmured, wondering what it was she was feeling. Somehow, with Reyn, it was hard to retain her composure.

His sharply defined eyebrows shot up in surprise. "I'm concerned about your health, Caitlin. Nothing more. I don't seduce teenagers."

Caitlin sighed, feeling more miserable with every passing minute. She let the remark about teenagers pass. She was just too sick to take offense. "It's just— I don't feel very comfortable about any of this. I don't know you. I shouldn't be here." She turned away from him, holding her arms tight to her chest, trying to keep the coldness at bay.

"Look, you're a friend of Gabby's," Reyn said from behind her. "The least I can do is give you a bit of help when you need it." He cupped her shoulders and swiveled her around to face him.

"And you don't need to worry about anything." Amusement lurked deep in his eyes. "I'll treat you exactly like I do Gabby." He grinned suddenly. "Well—maybe a little nicer. Okay?"

The grin softened his face and made him seem more approachable. For a fleeting second Caitlin longed to lean against him, to feel arms she was sure would be strong and comforting close around her. Surprised by the thought, she pulled away from his touch. "Okay," she said hoarsely, managing a brief smile. Feeling as she did, what choice did she have? She certainly wasn't up to leaving, not just now.

He showed her to the bathroom, insisting she take a hot bath. Caitlin didn't argue. Slipping into a tub full of hot water sounded heavenly. A shudder of anticipation ran through her. Maybe she would finally start to feel warm.

"Call me if you need anything," Reyn said as he shut the door behind himself.

Not likely, Caitlin thought, and quietly turned the lock. Was she doing the right thing? No matter how much Gabby had told her about Reyn, he was still a stranger—a handsome virile stranger. She felt uncomfortable knowing that he'd taken it upon himself to look after her, even if it was really Gabby to thank for his facade of concern.

For a moment she was tempted to fling the door open and leave, to return to the isolated comfort of her apartment. She wanted to be alone, not trapped here with Reyn. Realistically though, she knew she'd have to stay, at least for one night. Maybe after a good sleep she'd feel up to leaving. She didn't want to stay a moment longer than necessary.

Shoulders sagging with weariness, she went over to the tub and turned on the taps. Stripping quickly, she climbed into the tub, shuddering repeatedly as she eased her chilled body into the warmth. With a shaky sigh, she slid down, submerging to her chin. It felt so good.

When the water was as hot as she could stand it, she turned off the taps and lay back. Nice bathroom, she thought idly. It was large, done in shades of gray accented with navy blue and deep red. The tub was outsize and surrounded by a shelf of ceramic tile.

She wondered if Reyn used it often or if he was the type who only showered. Showered probably, she thought, thinking of the impatience he'd shown. As she stirred the water with her hand, she had a sudden disturbing picture of him stretched out in the tub, hot water steaming over his lithe body.

Frowning, Caitlin shook her head in irritation. It wasn't like her to think along these lines. It was enough that she was beginning to feel some sort of obligation toward Reyn. She didn't need to find him attractive, as well.

She felt cold again almost as soon as she left the water. After drying herself she realized she'd forgotten to bring any clean clothes in with her, and the sweat suit she'd been wearing lay in a damp crumpled heap on the floor. She picked it up, made a face of distaste, then folded it quickly. Shivering, she reached for the blue velour robe hanging on the back of the door and slipped it on, tying the belt tight around her waist and rolling up the sleeves. It felt soft and warm and smelled faintly of herbal soap. Part of her realized that it was too personal a garment for a stranger to borrow, but she was getting to the point where she didn't care anymore.

Reyn wasn't in sight when she came out, clutching her sweat suit against her. She looked cautiously down the hall, then made her way to the living room. It was empty. She walked quickly across the floor to the fireplace and sat on the raised hearth, holding her hands to the flames as she looked around.

Three steps led up from the living room to an eating area, which was separated from the kitchen by a breakfast counter. The living room itself was large. A comfortable-looking couch and a couple of chairs faced the fireplace while in front of the windows was the area Reyn obviously used for painting. There were shelves all along one wall, a drafting board pushed to one side and an easel set up in the middle, commanding a view of the outdoors.

Sketches and photographs were pinned to a corkboard, too distant for Caitlin to make out any details. Track lighting hung from a ceiling beam to illuminate the area.

Overflowing bookcases sat on each side of the huge stone fireplace. From what she could see, the books were varied, with paperbacks tucked among hardcover books, some new, some looking as though they had been read many times. In all, the room was warm and comfortable. Homey.

Caitlin leaned toward the fire, drying the ends of her hair. Where had Reyn gone? Her throat felt painfully dry and she longed for something hot to drink. A couple of aspirin wouldn't hurt, either.

He came down the hallway, the dog close on his heels.

Caitlin smoothed his robe over her knees and smiled nervously. "I borrowed your robe," she said. "My clothes were damp and I'd forgotten to take in any clean ones. I hope you don't mind."

He waved a hand dismissively. "Don't worry about it. Your suitcase is in the spare bedroom. You can change later. But first, I'll make you a hot drink. And something to eat, if you're hungry."

Caitlin shook her head quickly. Even if she had been hungry, she would have refused his offer of food. She was causing him enough trouble. A hot drink, however, was too tempting to turn down.

"A drink would be nice, thank you," she said, "but I couldn't eat."

"Right. One hot drink coming up." He went into the kitchen.

Caitlin kept a wary eye on the dog, but it flopped down on the floor a few feet away from her, resting its head on its paws, ears cocked in her direction. She turned from the strange blue eyes and huddled closer to the fire. The brief warmth she'd felt after her bath was long gone.

Reyn came back into the room carrying a mug. He handed it to her along with a couple of pills. "They're cold tablets," he said. "They'll cut that fever and help you sleep."

Caitlin glanced up at him with a tired smile of thanks. The mug contained hot milk sprinkled with nutmeg, and as she took a sip, she tasted a splash of brandy. It felt soothing to her raw throat. She swallowed the pills, wincing, and quickly drank more of the milk.

Reyn sat on the other side of the hearth, watching her finish the milk. "You're really feeling sick, aren't you?" he asked after a moment.

It was pointless to deny the obvious. Caitlin nodded, her lashes fanning her cheeks as she stared down at the mug in her hands. "I should be okay tomorrow," she said in a whisper, hoping she would be. Gabby's brother or not, he was still a stranger, and imposing on him went very much against the grain.

"Do you want me to call a doctor? There's one on the island—she's more or less retired, but she'll come over if there's a need."

Caitlin shook her head quickly. "It's just a cold."

"Are you sure it isn't something to do with your operation?"

"I'm sure." She glanced at him and managed a re-assuring smile. "Honest—it's only a cold. I just need to sleep it off."

"In that case, I'll show you to your room." He glanced at the mug. "Finished?"

She nodded and got to her feet, crossing her arms over her chest in an effort to keep the warmth of the fire with her. She'd be glad to get out of his way.

Reyn stared down at her. "You're a tiny little thing, aren't you?" His sudden smile was as unexpected as it was warm and he draped a friendly arm over her shoulders. "C'mon kid—let's get you to bed."

Caitlin let him lead her down the hall, too tired and sick to resent his touch. Surprisingly, she found it comforting, and didn't pull away as she normally would have.

"Here you go," he said, pushing open the door to a bedroom. "There are clean sheets on the bed and towels on the dresser. If you need anything, just let me know."

"I—I'm sorry to be so much trouble."

"Look. You're alone and you need help. I couldn't very well leave you to fend for yourself, could I?"

His words didn't make her feel a whole lot better. She knew she was intruding on his privacy, but at the moment there wasn't much she could do about it.

"Crawl into that bed and get some sleep," he ordered. "The thermostat is on the side—turn it up a couple of degrees if you feel cold."

"Thermostat?"

"It's a water bed," he explained.

"Oh." She blinked sleepily. "I've never slept on a water bed before. I'll probably get seasick on top of everything else."

"Don't you dare do that." Laughter lurked behind the mock horror in his voice. Chuckling, he left the room, shutting the door behind him.

Walking quietly across the carpeted floor, Caitlin pressed her ear to the door. She heard nothing on the other side. Once again she locked the door, then leaned against it for a moment wondering why she'd bothered. She might find Reyn attractive, but he made it pretty obvious that he saw her as little more than a nuisance foisted on him by his overly protective sister. That knowledge was enough to make her more determined than ever to leave first thing in the morning. She didn't want to be further indebted to Reyn Picard.

The cold tablets combined with the warm milk and brandy were starting to take effect. Her eyelids felt impossibly heavy and the bed beckoned enticingly. She rooted through her suitcase, found a pair of warm flannel pajamas and quickly put them on, then crawled into bed.

The warm water-filled mattress was incredibly comfortable. She tucked the corner of the pillow under her cheek and slept.

CHAPTER TWO

IT WAS EARLY MORNING when Caitlin awoke. She felt more clearheaded than she had the night before, but not by much. She stretched, then curled back up, stifling a groan. Her fever had dropped, but her throat was still scratchy and her eyes felt heavy and grainy. She'd have given anything to feel well again.

It was time to go home, but was she up to facing the trip back to Vancouver? She had to be! She didn't want to impose on Reyn Picard any longer. From what Gabby had said, his privacy was very important to him, and Caitlin could understand how an artist would need a lot of time to himself. It bothered her knowing she'd interrupted his work. She had no doubt that if she hadn't been so obviously sick, he would never have asked her into his home.

She rolled over and stared at the ceiling, wishing she could just slip out of the house and head home. She didn't want to see Reyn, to come face-to-face with his distracting presence only to have him treat her like a child he'd been saddled with.

But she had little choice at this point. She would eventually have to leave the room and go sit across from him at the breakfast table, trying to make polite conversation over the meal he'd undoubtedly insist on making. She grimaced a little at the thought of food. She still didn't have any appetite.

The house was quiet. She could hear the murmur of wind in the trees and the distant call of the ocean, but nothing else. From what she could see through the crack in the curtains, it was another dull cloudy day. Stretching again, she threw back the covers and somewhat reluctantly got out of bed.

She washed quickly, then dressed in jeans and a light blue sweatshirt. Standing before the mirror, she brushed her hair, glad she'd found the energy to get it cut before she'd left. Glossy bangs feathered across her forehead while the sides tapered to a blunt cut that curled under just above her shoulders.

Her hair might look all right, but the rest of her didn't. Her skin was still ashen. Ice-blue eyes, underlined by shadows, were strained and heavy-lidded. She looked tired and rundown. Sick. Like an abandoned child. Sighing, she put down the brush and turned away from the mirror.

After making the bed, she opened the door and peered cautiously down the hallway.

She saw no sign of Reyn as she walked quietly into the living room, but the dog lay on the rug in front of the fireplace. Its head shot up as it sensed her presence and it scrambled to its feet, slinking away from her. That suited Caitlin fine. She went into the kitchen.

It was a well-appointed room, bright and welcoming even on a dark and gloomy morning. Almond-colored appliances gleamed when she turned on the overhead light, as did the tidy blue-tiled countertops. A coffee maker sat on one counter, filled and ready to be switched on. Caitlin did so and heard the gurgle of heating water. A cup of coffee would taste great, she thought as she wandered back into the living room waiting for it to brew.

The dog had gone back to its spot in front of the fireplace, so Caitlin crossed to stand by the window. The misty rain hid most of the view, but she suspected it would be spectacular on a clear day.

It was a beautiful place, and the relative isolation would be perfect for an artist, but it wouldn't do for her, at least not for long. Her life was in the city, close to the children who needed her help.

The aroma of freshly brewed coffee wafted from the kitchen. Circling the dog who watched her with his strange blue eyes, Caitlin went to pour herself a cup. She was sitting back at the window when Reyn came into the room, dressed in jeans and a sweatshirt, worn moccasins on his feet.

Caitlin smiled shyly, acutely aware of how handsome he was. Nothing that Gabby had told her had quite prepared her for it. "Good morning," she said quietly. "The coffee's just ready."

Reyn nodded abruptly as he smoothed a palm over his damp hair. "Good. Are you feeling any better this morning?" he asked on his way into the kitchen.

"Better, thanks," she assured him, wondering if he'd believe her. The mirror hadn't lied. She didn't look any better than she felt.

He eyed her thoughtfully when he returned, but said nothing more than, "That's good." He sat down and took a sip from his steaming mug, then looked at her positioned near the window and then at the dog on the hearth.

"I see you're still scared of Rex."

"It's silly, I know," Caitlin said quickly, hearing the mocking tone behind his words. "I don't like being afraid, but..." She shrugged apologetically. "I'm not bad with little dogs, but Rex is kind of big. And his eyes—they're so strange."

"He's a husky," Reyn told her. "Many of them have blue eyes."

"Have you had him long?" She might not like the dog, but it was something to talk about.

"About two years. I found him on the side of the highway when I was returning from Victoria one rainy winter day. He was curled up on the shoulder, soaking wet and shivering—a lost little puppy. I thought he'd been hit by a car at first, but couldn't find anything wrong with him. Either he'd gotten himself lost or someone had dumped him there to get rid of him. Whatever happened, it's left him very wary of strangers, for all his friendliness."

He grinned unexpectedly. "Like I said, he's probably just as afraid of you as you are of him. Now—what would you like for breakfast?"

In spite of her insistence that she wasn't hungry, Reyn made her a plate of scrambled eggs and toast. The food was tasty and the first few mouthfuls went down fine, then her throat seemed to close and she couldn't take another bite.

"Is that all you're going to eat?" Reyn asked, frowning at her from across the breakfast counter as she pushed her plate away.

"I'm just not very hungry," she said, glancing at him, then away again quickly, feeling suddenly very

tired and a little dizzy. She put an elbow on the edge
of the counter and rested her head on her hand.

"I'm sorry," she whispered miserably. "I guess I'm
still not feeling all that well."

"I didn't think so. Go lie down," he ordered.
"Sleep for a while. You look like you need a good rest
as much as anything."

She hated her dependency on Reyn. It made her
think of her mother's continual reliance on men in her
futile attempts to improve her life. Caitlin's frustra-
tion over the situation showed in her eyes and she
caught Reyn looking at her. "I wanted to go home today," she murmured, standing up.

"Caitlin, relax," Reyn said firmly. "You may as
well stay, now that you're here."

He stopped her as she moved past him, placing a
cool hand on her brow, smiling a bit as she ducked out
from under his touch.

"Relax," he said again, his deep voice rich with
amusement. "I'm concerned about your health, that's
all. Believe me, I'm not about to start seducing you."

Color suffused her pale cheeks. "I wasn't thinking
that," she said stiffly, crossing her arms over her chest
as she turned away from the laughter in his eyes.

"Good," he murmured, his lips twitching as she
glanced back at him. "Now, go lie down for a while."

With an abrupt nod, Caitlin left for the bedroom.
He was laughing at her, and she wished fervently she'd
stood still under his touch. Ducking away had been an
instinctive reaction. Except for the children she
worked with, she didn't like being touched. The sensation of Reyn's hand on her brow hadn't felt imper-
sonal. Not to her. It was a disturbing thought.

With a sigh, she pulled off her jeans and crawled into the bed she'd just recently made. The water-filled mattress seemed to envelop her, giving warmth and comfort. Pulling the covers snug around her neck, she closed her eyes. An image of Reyn's face came to her, unbidden.

It was a handsome sensitive face with a strong set jaw and a deep line that contradicted his dreamy artist's eyes. Gabby had said he was good-looking. She hadn't been wrong.

She'd told Caitlin a lot about him. It felt strange, meeting someone for the first time and already knowing a lot of intimate details of his life. He wouldn't be pleased, Caitlin was sure. He was a self-contained, private man. She needed no one to tell her that.

Reyn's father was married to Gabby's mother. The two families had become one when Reyn was about fifteen, Gabby ten and her sister, Jackie, a couple of years older. Gabby said that she and Jackie had adored Reyn right from the start. He was a wonderful big brother.

He was an artist even then, to the chagrin of his father who would have preferred his son to follow a more traditional career. It bothered him that Reyn wanted to study nature and paint rather than play hockey or other sports. According to Gabby, they'd fought a lot, her stepfather unable to accept Reyn for what he was.

He was a fine artist. Caitlin had seen enough of his work to know that. He put more than a photographic rendering of wildlife to canvas. It was the exquisite detail and texture, the depths to his paintings that made them special, and he was rapidly gaining world-wide acclaim.

Caitlin rolled onto her side and stared blindly out the window. According to Gabby, he also had a reputation with women. Not for one-night stands, Gabby said. His affairs usually lasted several months, often drifting into lasting friendships. Gabby didn't think he'd ever gotten over his first love.

Reyn had met Tamara when he was eighteen. She was several years older, an artist, as well. She had him by the hormones, Gabby had said, quoting her stepfather as she told the story with her usual exuberance and in exhaustive detail. They'd moved in together and married shortly afterward. And four years later, when she'd left him for someone else, Reyn had been devastated.

"He's never gotten over it," Gabby had told her. "Not really. Y'know, most of his girlfriends since then have looked like Tamara—tall and curvy, with wild blondish hair."

Caitlin smiled a little ruefully as she remembered Gabby's words. If that was the how he liked his women, he wasn't going to notice her. It was probably just as well, she told herself, but part of her couldn't help but wonder what it would be like to be desired by a man like Reyn.

SLOWLY CAITLIN BECAME AWARE of the mattress rolling gently under her, of another presence in the room. Her dark fan of lashes lifted from her cheeks and she inhaled sharply. Reyn was sitting on the bed.

Startled, Caitlin stared up at him, her eyes wide. "W-what?"

There was a smile in his voice as though her wariness amused him. "Supper's ready, kid," he said, standing up. "Come and get it. Five minutes," he added over his shoulder and left the room.

Feeling heavy-headed and still tired, Caitlin made her way to the bathroom. She splashed warm water on her face and dragged a comb through her sleep-tangled hair. It didn't help much. She still looked washed out and tired. With a halfhearted shrug, she turned away from the mirror and headed for the kitchen.

Reyn had set the dining table, and the warm smell of good cooking filled the air. There was a fire burning in the grate, and the curtains had been drawn against the cold November night. But the crackle of the fire couldn't hide the sound of wind-driven rain spattering against the windows.

Reyn turned from the stove, a platter of chicken in his hand. "Just in time. Have a seat," he said, inclining his head toward the table.

Skirting the dog cautiously, Caitlin pulled out a chair and sat, hoping she'd be able to do justice to the meal.

The boneless chicken had been breaded and seasoned with oregano and garlic before being baked. As well, there were stuffed baked potatoes and broccoli with cheese sauce. A bottle of wine sat open and ready to pour.

"This looks very good," Caitlin commented as she slid a potato onto her plate. "Do you cook like this all the time?"

"Off and on." He shrugged. "It depends on how busy I am."

"Are you painting right now?" She hoped he wasn't. She'd hate to think that she'd interrupted his concentration.

"I've been working on a series of bald eagles, but I took a couple of days off to tend to some business in Victoria. That's where I was when Gabby phoned. Otherwise I would have told her it wasn't a very good idea." He cut into his chicken and took a bite.

"I'm sorry," Caitlin said stiffly. "I wouldn't have come, but Gabby insisted it would be all right."

"Gabby's full of great ideas, but she never stops to think things through. She should have realized how uncomfortable that cabin would be at this time of the year, especially for someone who's been sick. As it is, she's been phoning every five minutes to make sure you're all right."

Caitlin pushed a piece of chicken across her plate, wishing more than ever that she hadn't listened to Gabby. Reyn had felt obliged to take her in and that bothered her, left her feeling in his debt.

Reyn picked up the wine bottle. "Would you like some?"

Caitlin hesitated. She didn't drink much, but maybe a glass of wine would help her relax. She still felt awkward and uncomfortable. "Yes, please," she said. "Just a bit." He poured them both a glass and she took a sip. It was dry and cool, just the way she liked it.

"It's lovely," she said. "And so is the food. You're a good cook." It was true. She just wished she had more appetite. As it was, she had to force herself to swallow.

"Thanks." His smile was slow and lazy, but his deep brown eyes missed nothing. "You don't have to eat any more if you're full," he said. "I promise not to be offended."

"I'm sorry. I just don't seem to be hungry these days." She put down her knife and fork and took another sip of the wine.

"You really do need to try and eat more, though. You're too thin."

Caitlin blushed a little at his directness but didn't let it get to her. "I lose weight a lot easier than I gain it," she said with a little shrug. "And I'm not much of a cook. It's easier to make a sandwich or a salad."

"Isn't there some nice young man eager to take care of you?" he asked teasingly.

Frowning in irritation, Caitlin rubbed a finger over the stem of her wineglass. "I don't need a man to look after me. I'm an adult, Mr. Picard, and quite capable of taking care of myself."

"Are you now?" he asked, amused by the look on her face. Then he changed the subject abruptly. "How long have you known Gabby?"

Caitlin smothered her resentment and replied, "Since last spring, when she took over the grade-two class at our school."

"What grade do you teach?"

"It's a class of children with emotional problems. There are eight kids, all at different levels."

"That must be quite hectic."

A sudden smile lit her face. "Hectic is too mild a word. Most days, it borders on chaotic." Her expression became serious again. "But in their own ways, they're great kids, all of them."

"You care a lot about them, don't you?"

Caitlin hid most of her emotions from the world, but not how she felt about the children she worked with. She nodded decisively.

"So," Reyn said, "instead of enjoying your unexpected time off, you're champing at the bit."

Caitlin glanced at him with a quick smile and nodded again. "I hate being out of the classroom. It's hard on the kids. They'd just gotten used to me again after being home all summer, then this happened. And by the time they get used to the sub, I'll be back. But—" she sighed "—it can't be helped."

"What made you want to work with problem kids? A regular class must be a lot easier."

"It is," Caitlin answered, frowning a bit as she tried to explain. "But there are so many kids who just can't cope in regular classes. My class may seem undisciplined on the surface, but it's actually quite structured. The kids really need firm guidelines, but at the same time, they need to be free to work out the anger—or pain—most of them have. I can't fix what's wrong in their lives, but I can teach them ways to cope with it."

Reyn rested his elbows on the table, watching her face as she spoke. The taut tired air was gone, and a sparkle chased the coolness from her eyes.

She blushed again when she caught his look. She knew that, for perhaps the first time, he was seeing her as someone other than his sister's sick—young—friend. It gave her a funny feeling. Pushing back her chair, she picked up her plate. "I'll clean up," she offered hastily, feeling as though she'd been babbling. As a rule she was a listener, not a talker.

"Leave it," Reyn said firmly, standing up. "Take your wine over to the fire and relax. I'll make some . . . tea? Coffee?"

"Tea would be nice, please. But let me help."

"It'll only take me a couple of minutes to put things in the dishwasher. Go sit down," he ordered, stacking plates.

Caitlin did as he said, settling herself onto the couch opposite the fire. The flames had died to glowing embers, but it was still warm. She sipped her wine, watching as the dog padded into the kitchen and sat in the middle of the floor, his hopeful eyes on the plates.

"Want some food, Rex?" Reyn asked.

The dog's tail swept the pale blue tiles as his ears went back and he whined deep in his throat. He squirmed anxiously as Reyn scraped pieces of chicken into a large yellow bowl in a corner of the room.

"Okay, boy—it's all yours."

The dog was across the floor in a flash, burying his nose deep in the bowl as he gobbled the leftovers. Reyn cast a quick glance at Caitlin, then stooped to rub the dog's ears. "How can anyone be afraid of a goofy guy like you?"

Caitlin smiled a little as she looked back at the fireplace. She swallowed the last of her wine, then relaxed into the corner of the couch.

She felt warm and very much at ease. *It must be the wine,* she thought. The clink and clatter of dishes faded into the background and she stared at the dying embers of the fire. She was tired again, the brief spark of energy dulled. Her head ached and she rested it on the crook of her arm. Her eyelids drooped, then shut, and she slept.

She felt an arm slide under her neck, another under her knees, and then she was being lifted. She blinked and frowned into the dark eyes so close to hers. "Put me down," she said, her voice husky with sleep.

"Relax, kid." Reyn's teeth flashed white as he grinned down at her. "I'll tuck you into bed, then I'll leave you alone. I promise."

Caitlin felt vaguely surprised at herself for not struggling, not demanding to be put down. It just seemed too much trouble, and there was nothing threatening about the feel of his arms around her, or the scrape of his shirt under her cheek as her head rested against his shoulder. Even his warm male scent was somehow reassuring. *It must be the wine,* she thought again with a sleepy sigh, but knew it wasn't. Half-asleep or not, she was very aware of her attraction to him.

He placed her gently on the bed. She stared up at him, her eyes luminous in the half-light. "I'm going home tomorrow," she murmured.

His lean fingers touched her cheek fleetingly. "We'll talk about it in the morning. Night, kid."

Caitlin watched through sleepy eyes as he left the room, shutting the door quietly. She pulled up the covers and rolled onto her side, luxuriating in the warmth. *I could learn to like him,* she thought. *A lot.* Too tired to think about him any longer, she drifted off.

ALL THE SLEEP she'd had over the past couple of days had worked wonders. Caitlin woke up feeling rested and well for the first time in a long time. She showered quickly, styled her hair with her blow dryer and dressed in jeans and a thick cream-colored sweater.

Reyn was seated in the living room, drinking coffee as he read a paper, his long jean-clad legs propped up on the table in front of him. A radio played softly in the background. "Good morning," he said, looking up as she came into the room. He wore dark-framed reading glasses that managed to make him seem even more attractive.

"Good morning," Caitlin murmured.

"Coffee's ready." He gestured toward the kitchen. "Help yourself."

Caitlin poured herself a cup, then returned to the living room. She sat in the armchair farthest from the dog.

Reyn folded his paper and put it down. "How are you feeling this morning?" he asked.

"Much better, thanks." Caitlin took a sip of coffee. "I'll be able to go home today."

Reyn removed his glasses and laid them on the end table beside his coffee mug. "I wanted to talk to you about that—"

"Really—I'm all right now," Caitlin interjected quickly. "There's a ferry leaving around twelve-thirty, isn't there? I'll catch that one."

"I'd like you to stay for a while longer, Caitlin."

Caitlin shook her head. "I'm okay," she repeated. "Honestly. I should get home."

"I want to paint you," he said abruptly.

Caitlin's eyes widened in surprise and she stared at him. "Paint me?"

He nodded. "I've got a couple of ideas. I want to paint you with Rex—there's a resemblance I'd like to bring out."

Fine brows arched over cool ice-blue eyes. "Let me get this straight—you want to paint me because I look like a dog?"

Reyn gave a rich chuckle. "Far from it—a little lost kitten, maybe. A dog, never. I'm talking about the coloring, the eyes especially. And your hair has a reddish tint, not unlike Rex's fur. Your coloring is quite striking." He nodded, his eyes narrowing thoughtfully. "I think it could work."

Caitlin shook her head. "No, Reyn. I can't stay any longer. I've got to get back."

"Why?" he asked bluntly. "You planned on staying at the cabin for more than a couple of days, didn't you? And I assume you have plenty of sick time left."

"Just under a month. But—"

"I'm serious about wanting to paint you, Caitlin," he interrupted. "You've got nothing else to do, right?"

She shook her head.

"I've lost my interest in eagles for the moment. I'm ready to try something else. You've given me a couple of ideas I'd like to work through. Come on—you can spare me some time. Don't you think you owe me one?"

"I thought you were a wildlife artist." She didn't want to succumb to the feeling of obligation growing in her.

He shrugged. "I'm always ready to try something different. Besides, Rex looks kind of wild." They both glanced over at the dog who lay flopped on his back, paws dangling while he snored softly.

"Sometimes," Reyn rectified, grinning broadly. "So, how about it, kid? I'd really like to give it a try."

Caitlin looked down into her mug, frowning slightly with indecision. Basically, all she wanted to do was return to Vancouver as quickly as possible. But she had distracted Reyn from his work and did feel she owed him something. He seemed sincere about wanting to paint her, for whatever reason. *And he's certainly not going to come on to you,* she thought wryly, conscious of a faint sense of disappointment. A man who thought of her as a lost little kitten and called her "kid" obviously did *not* find her attractive. It was a disturbing thought. She glanced at him sideways.

"Are you sure?"

He nodded. "I'm sure."

"Then...I guess I'll stay. For a couple of days, anyway." She didn't owe him any more than that.

"Good," Reyn said with satisfaction. "Now that that's settled, let's eat. What would you like for breakfast? And don't tell me you aren't hungry. You must be starving by now."

"I am kind of hungry," she admitted. "What I would really like is some toast and peanut butter, if you have it." She saw his look of amused indulgence and immediately wished she'd asked for something else.

"I usually keep a jar on hand for Jackie's daughter, Nicole. Like most kids, she lives on the stuff." He picked up his mug and got to his feet. "Let's go take a look."

Caitlin followed him into the kitchen already regretting that she'd agreed to stay, but it would be awkward to back out now. Surely it wouldn't take more than a couple of days for him to get what he wanted. Her obligation, such as it was, would be fulfilled and she could return to Vancouver and resume the life she'd chosen for herself.

As Caitlin sat at the breakfast counter nibbling a piece of toast, she examined the painting on the wall in the dining area. At first glance it appeared to be a rock face, richly textured and patterned with subtly colored lichens. Roots from the barely glimpsed trees at the top of the painting crept down jagged cracks in the granite surface. A closer look showed a bird clinging to a feathered green branch off to one side.

Frowning a bit, Caitlin tilted her head and looked again. Some of the cracks began to form patterns. She saw what could be a deer, a fishlike animal and an elongated human form superimposed over the others, yet fading into the overall picture.

She turned to Reyn with a smile of appreciation. "That's a marvelous painting. There's such a lot of interesting detail. I get the feeling that every time I look at it, I'm going to see something different."

"You saw the pictographs then."

She nodded. "They really add something. Is that an actual setting?"

He shook his head. "It's two or three settings made into one—as are most of my paintings. I try to make them my own. I've come across a number of pictographs, all across Canada, actually. I liked the idea of blending them with the patterns on the rock surface.

"I like it," Caitlin said. "What kind of bird is that?"

"It's a western towhee. Or, as my grandfather used to call them, a swamp robin."

Caitlin looked away from the painting and added a little more milk to her coffee. "Did your grandfather live around here?"

"On the Island, in the Comox Valley," Reyn answered. He reached for another piece of toast and slathered it with blackberry jam. "He was a logger and a trapper at times—whatever it took to make a living. I spent a lot of time with him in the forest when I was a boy. He's responsible for my love of nature."

"It comes through in your paintings."

"I hope so. I want people to appreciate the riches we have in nature and join the fight to preserve them. It's damn close to being too late."

"Gabby said you were quite the conservationist."

"Oh, yeah?" Reyn said, arching his brows. "And what else did she say about me?"

"Absolutely nothing," Caitlin denied quickly, fighting back a smile. "Your name was hardly ever mentioned."

"I'll bet," Reyn said dryly. He stood up. "Let's get these dishes cleared away and get started on some sketches."

Caitlin rose reluctantly. She had her doubts about the whole thing, but she'd go along with him if that's what it took to repay him for taking her out of that dank little cabin and into his home. He probably wouldn't go very far with his idea of painting her, she told herself. And that would suit her just fine. Reyn's presence was unsettling. She had a feeling that the sooner she returned home, the better.

CHAPTER THREE

By MIDAFTERNOON some of the surprise Caitlin felt at Reyn's request had worn off. But she still wondered at how easily she'd gone along with his intimation that she owed him for taking her in. She should feel some resentment, shouldn't she?

And yet the question really on her mind was why he'd want to paint her in the first place. The thought of sitting still under his artistic scrutiny made her uneasy.

"I'll need to make some preliminary sketches," Reyn informed her. "But first things first—come over here and make friends with Rex."

Caitlin did as he asked, not averse to overcoming her lingering childhood fear. She'd laid other ones to rest. Why not this one? She glanced at Reyn and the gleam of withheld laughter in his eyes made her stiffen her resolve. No way was she going to react like the child he persisted in thinking her.

The dog sat beside his master, looking up at Caitlin, ears pricked and eyes alert. Tentatively, she held out her hand, keeping still while the dog sniffed it.

"It's his eyes," she murmured. "It seems like he's always staring at me." She suppressed a shudder. She'd had nightmares about dogs with staring eyes.

"You notice his eyes because we expect a dog's eyes to be brown. Once you get used to the color, it won't seem so bad. And he's not sure about you, so he's watching you more than usual. Go on—pat him. It won't hurt."

The dog's tail made a hesitant sweep over the floor as she rubbed the fur between his ears.

"What happened?" asked Reyn. "Did you get bitten, or were you just frightened?"

"I was frightened," Caitlin answered briefly. Terrified was a better word, she thought, not only by the dog, but by the sly cruelties of her mother's lover.

The dog bumped his nose against her hand, then swiped at it with his tongue. Caitlin kept herself from flinching and continued to rub the soft warm fur.

She looked up at Reyn with a little smile. "I guess he's not so bad." She straightened, wiping her hand on her jeans. "But I don't think I'll ever get used to dog spit."

Reyn chuckled, his eyes narrow with laughter. "I won't ask you to. Now—do you think you'll be able to bear having him sit beside you while I do some sketching?"

"I still think this is a crazy idea, but..." She shrugged. If he really wanted to do it, she wouldn't object.

SHE WAS UNCOMFORTABLE at first, acutely aware of Reyn as his narrowed eyes scrutinized her face. The line between his brows cut deep, giving him a distant, cold look.

When he crossed to where she was sitting, frowning as he took her chin between his thumb and forefinger and tilted her face toward the light, she had to fight an urge to pull away. She reminded herself that there was nothing personal about his touch. She couldn't say the same about the way his fingers made *her* feel. Her heartbeat quickened and a slow flush stained her cheeks.

"You have a nice face." His deep voice was thoughtful as his fingers traced the line from the curve of her chin to her cheekbones. "Almost heart-shaped . . . and your eyes are like a cat's. Kitten's," he amended. "A cat shows more self-assurance. You're really quite shy, aren't you?" he asked suddenly.

Caitlin's lashes lifted from her cheeks and she looked at him directly, fighting for composure. "Yes—and this doesn't help."

He laughed and removed his hand, stepping back as he did so. "You'll get used to it. It's a little like having your picture taken. One shot makes you feel self-conscious, but after several you begin to relax." He grinned. "Just think of me as a camera and I'll blend into the background."

He was too vibrant a man to ever blend into the background. Caitlin doubted that she would ever really relax under the glint of those knowing eyes. It would take a lot to prevent him from seeing the feelings he was unwittingly stirring within her.

"What do you want me to do?"

He shrugged. "Nothing really. Just sit on that chair by the window. Read if you want."

Eventually she was able to make sense out of the jumble of words in her book, although she wasn't able to completely dismiss Reyn from her mind. She was very aware of him sitting at his drafting table, his eyes sharp with concentration as his lean fingers sketched her image.

When he finally tossed down his charcoal and stretched, she felt the tension drain from her muscles and sighed softly with relief.

"That wasn't so bad, was it?" he asked, taking off his glasses. The sharp line of concentration cutting his brow seemed less pronounced.

Caitlin marked her place in her book and closed it, shaking her head in answer.

"Good, because I think this is going to work. Really work," he said thoughtfully, staring at the papers in front of him. He looked up and smiled, abstraction fleeing from his eyes. "Feeling a bit stiff?"

Caitlin nodded. "A bit."

"I'm going for a walk. You can come if you want."

Caitlin glanced out the window. The day was dull gray and blurred with mist, but the thought of a walk held immense appeal, even if his offer had been somewhat less than enthusiastic. It seemed a long time since she'd been outside.

"I'd love to," she said, putting her book down and standing up. "I'll get my coat."

THE AIR WAS THICK and moist, perfumed with cedar. It embraced the skin and clung, beading into tiny drops. Caitlin raised her head and breathed deep, her eyes half-closed with pleasure. It felt wonderful. She turned to Reyn and smiled. "Which way do we go?"

He jerked his head to the right. "That way. We'll go down to the beach."

With the dog bounding excitedly before them, they walked through the trees to a path skirting the edge of the cliff.

The land sloped gradually to a wide curve of sandy bay rimmed by gray beached logs, sleek and shiny with rain. Quiet waves left a trace of lacy foam on the sand as the water pushed its way back into the bay.

Caitlin walked beside Reyn, hands deep in the pockets of her jacket. She glanced at him occasionally but said nothing, sensing that his thoughts were elsewhere. His strong chin was raised high as he strode along the wet sand and his eyes held a distant dreamy look. He was painting in his mind, she thought, and quickened her pace to keep up with him.

The dog, nose to the ground, ran erratically between the beached logs, then veered abruptly to disappear among the trees. Farther along the shore, a few gulls waded in frothy water, pecking at a clump of debris. When they suddenly took flight with raucous squawks of protest, Reyn stopped, raising his hand. As Caitlin came up beside him, a bald eagle glided out of the mist. Talons extended, it swooped down and grabbed the gulls' meal, carrying it aloft with lazy strokes of its wings.

"Thief," Caitlin murmured.

"Opportunist," Reyn stated, watching the eagle disappear. He turned and looked at her upturned face. "You're wet," he said, sounding surprised.

"So are you." Moisture glistened on his skin and hair, deepening the dark waves into loose curls.

"We should go back."

She shook her head quickly. "I'm fine. Really."

"You've been sick, Caitlin. I don't want you getting chilled. We'll go back."

Ignoring her frown of protest at his arbitrary decision, he put two fingers in his mouth and whistled shrilly. Within seconds the dog appeared, bounding toward them, his fur soaked. As he reached them, he skidded to a stop and shook violently, then began to prance happily, whining deep in his throat.

"Let's go home, boy," Reyn urged, and the dog leapt ahead, nose to the ground once more. "See? Even he has the sense to know when it's time to come in out of the rain." He grinned teasingly, his eyes flashing.

Caitlin sighed in mock exasperation and shook her head. She found it hard to stay annoyed with Reyn. Turning away from the appealing light in his deep brown eyes, she watched the dog lead the way home.

"He really likes this," she said.

"Even more than sleeping and eating." Reyn began the trek back, his long legs carrying him quickly toward the house. Caitlin had to hurry to keep up with him.

AN OPEN BOOK rested forgotten on her knees as Caitlin gazed out the window, thinking how comfortable she'd become during the past few days. It continued to surprise her just how easy it was to be with Reyn, even though at times he seemed distant and moody. She put such moments down to artistic temperament and refused to let them bother her.

Even his constant scrutiny as he sketched her ceased to cause discomfort. She'd become used to knowing those deep brown eyes were on her face, her body, slowly coming to understand that there was nothing personal in it; he was intent on capturing her image, nothing more.

And slowly they were becoming friends. The knowledge was like a warm little glow inside, and she hugged it to herself, a smile playing on her lips. She'd spent much of her life alone, with almost no family to speak of. She knew the real value of friendship. And friendship with someone like Reyn—handsome, compelling and very male—was something new. And intriguing.

"What are you thinking?"

Reyn's deep voice startled her, and she turned abruptly, her eyes wide. Smiling, she shook her head. "Nothing much. But you were right—I hardly notice you any more." That was a bit of a lie. She might feel more comfortable in his presence, but she was always aware of him.

"Starting to blend into the background, am I?"

"Just part of the furniture," she agreed, stretching a little. "Are you finished?"

He nodded, sitting back on the stool, unwinding his legs from the rungs. "I'm about ready to start painting. I want to do more than one," he added unexpectedly. "I need you to stay longer."

Caitlin had fully expected to return to Vancouver within a couple of days. "I don't think I should," she said slowly. "I've been here over a week already."

"But you're comfortable here, aren't you?"

She nodded.

"And there's no reason for you to hurry back, is there?"

"No," she answered slowly. "Not really."

"Then stay," he prompted. "After wolves, cougars and eagles, I'm finding a human face interesting. I'd like to explore it further."

"You said I owed you one," she said. "You've got one."

"I've changed my mind—you owe me two."

"Reyn—"

"I'd like you to stay, Caitlin. I'm serious about this."

She could tell that he was. And after all, she *had* interrupted his series on the eagles—maybe she did owe him a bit more of her time. "How much longer would you want me to stay?"

He shrugged. "Until you have to return to work." He grinned, his teeth flashing white. "I'm enjoying the company, as much as anything."

Caitlin felt a mixture of surprise and pleasure. "I thought artists were solitary people."

"I hardly notice you're here," he said. "You're—"

"Part of the furniture," she finished dryly, wondering if it would always be that way.

His eyes sparked with laughter. "I was going to say a quiet little thing, but I guess that doesn't sound much better. It makes you sound drab and uneventful. You're not that."

"Thank you."

He grinned. "You're welcome. What I mean to say is that you're a—a restful person. You don't feel the need to fill every moment with action or talk. There's an air of peace about you. Gabby would have driven me up one wall and down another by now, with her mouth going a hundred miles an hour."

"I won't tell her you said so."

Reyn laughed. "I've told her myself. That's one of the reasons I had that cabin built. I can always send her there when I need some peace and quiet. So...want to go for a walk?"

Caitlin did, but she shook her head. "Not today, thanks. You go ahead." She had the feeling Reyn was shortening his walks because of her. They never went very far before he suggested turning back, and she could never figure out if he was afraid she'd get tired— or if he was simply tired of her company.

"I think I will," he said, standing up and stretching his lithe lean body. "Rex, want to go for a walk?"

The dog leapt up, whining, and ran to Reyn, squirming excitedly around his feet. Laughing, Reyn got his jacket and went to the door. "Okay, boy, let's go. See you in a while," he added to Caitlin, raising his hand.

When he'd gone, Caitlin decided to walk to the point. She put on her coat and went outside, noting as she made her way there the low clouds that still covered the sky, their wispy bottoms catching in the tree-tops.

Caitlin crouched on the edge of land, looking into the ocean rolling ceaselessly onto the rocks below. Glancing up, she could see only clouds where the mainland mountains should have been. A tugboat plowed through the gray waters of the strait, towing a barge toward Vancouver. Shivering in the damp air, she moved back to sit on a rock.

Reyn wanted her to stay. She hadn't given him an answer, but her silence implied that she would. Did she want to?

Caitlin nibbled on a thumbnail, her eyes thoughtful. He really seemed to want to paint her, and now
that she felt comfortable with the idea, she found it
flattering. Reyn Picard was a famous artist and he
wanted to paint *her*.

It wouldn't hurt to stay, would it?

Caitlin frowned. In spite of Reyn's abrupt manner
and irritating habit of thinking of her as another kid
sister, she found much about him to like. And as her
liking grew, so did another unexpected feeling. She
was becoming very aware of him in a physical sense.
The feeling was new to her.

Caitlin considered herself an oddity. In all of her
twenty-five years, she'd never been really attracted to
a man. There was nothing wrong with her sexuality,
she was certain; it was just that she had never met a
man she wanted as other than a friend. And even if she
had, unless she knew for certain that he wanted a permanent relationship, she wouldn't succumb.

Caitlin sighed. She didn't want to be like her
mother. She didn't want the dalliances with which
Janet had cluttered her life. Before Caitlin allowed a
man into *her* life, she needed to know he was going to
stay.

So she had to be realistic about her growing attraction to Reyn. He didn't return what she was beginning to feel. That was obvious. Oh, he liked her well
enough. He seemed to enjoy her company and, whatever his reasons, he wanted to paint her. But not once
had she detected any kind of spark from him, no sense
of sexual awareness. She was his kid sister's friend and
that was as far as it went.

Caitlin dug her heel into the thick layer of evergreen needles covering the ground. Friendship was all she could expect from Reyn, and that was just as well. Her time on the island was temporary, a brief respite from the real world.

REYN MADE ENCHILADAS when he returned from his walk. As they sat down to eat, the gray daylight deepened into dusk. Firelight flickered warmly in the stone hearth and soft music filled the room.

"I just realized you didn't give me an answer this afternoon," Reyn said suddenly.

Caitlin looked up from spooning sour cream onto her plate. "About what?" she asked, passing him the container.

"About staying. Will you?"

Caitlin hesitated. She'd pretty well decided that maybe it would be best if she returned to Vancouver.

"Say yes, Caitlin," Reyn insisted. "I want you to stay."

And *I* want to stay, she admitted silently. Surely it would do no harm. She was aware of her feelings for Reyn, and just as aware that he didn't return them. Realistically, there was no problem, as long as she remained clearheaded about things. She should be able to manage that. She always had.

"Well?"

Caitlin glanced around the room, conscious of its warm welcoming atmosphere, then met Reyn's eyes. She gave a rueful shrug. She still sensed she should leave, but it was easy to talk herself into staying. "If you're sure . . ."

"I am."

She sighed. "Okay. I'll stay. But just a few more days," she added hastily.

Reyn nodded with satisfaction. "Good." Unexpectedly he held out his hand. "Between us, we'll make great paintings." He grinned at her.

Cautiously Caitlin laid her hand in his, feeling the vibrancy in his strong warm fingers as they closed around hers. "You're the artist," she said, pulling her tingling hand from his. It amazed her that such a simple touch could arouse so much feeling.

He was looking at her through thoughtful eyes. "Only if I can capture you—your essence. The person I sense inside."

Caitlin forced her eyes from his and looked down at her plate, her heartbeat quickening. She knew then that she didn't have as much control over her emotions as she'd thought. And for a brief moment, she didn't really care.

AFTER SHOWERING and blow-drying her hair, Caitlin went into the kitchen to switch on the coffee maker. As usual, she was up before Reyn. He stayed awake later than she did and slept longer in the morning.

As the coffee brewed, she opened the door to let Rex out. She still didn't feel entirely comfortable around the dog, but she didn't go out of her way to avoid him as she had at the beginning.

By the time she'd poured herself a mug of coffee, Rex was back, wanting to be let in. Caitlin obliged, shutting the door quickly against the chill damp air. The dog trotted to his usual place near the fireplace. Another dull day, she thought, standing at the window, sipping her coffee. It seemed a long time since she'd seen the sun.

Turning away from the window, she bumped against the small table holding her books. The top ones slid off the pile and hit the floor with a sharp slapping sound.

The dog leapt to his feet and cringed, tail tucked between his legs and ears laid flat against his head. He cowered, watching Caitlin through wary blue eyes.

Caitlin saw the fear in him and responded the way she would to a frightened child. She walked slowly toward him, speaking in a low soothing voice.

"Hey—it's okay, Rex. It's just a bit of noise." She held out her hand to him and he cautiously sniffed it and gave a tentative wag of his tail. Caitlin crouched down beside him, gently stroking his head. "It's okay, boy. I won't hurt you."

She hated to see fear, even in a dog. He started to relax as she patted him gently; then he lay down, resting his muzzle on her knees and gazing soulfully up at her. Caitlin smiled, warming to the dog for the first time.

"You're not so bad, are you?" she murmured, scratching him behind one ear. She laughed at the look of bliss on his face and scratched a little harder. "You're just a big old teddy bear."

"That's what I've been trying to tell you."

Startled, Caitlin looked across the room at Reyn. He was leaning against the wall of the hallway, smiling at her, his hair damp from the shower.

She found it hard not to stare. Somehow, impossibly, he was even more appealing than usual. She wanted to touch him. Averting her eyes, she strove to keep her tone light.

"I finally realized that he was more afraid of me than I was of him," she said.

"Does that mean you're going to be friends at last?"

Caitlin looked at the dog, then back at Reyn. "As long as he doesn't drool on me."

"Good. That should work well with the second painting I have in mind."

Caitlin gave the dog a final pat and stood. "Just how many do you plan on doing?"

Reyn straightened up and shrugged. "I've got a couple of ideas I want to try. I'll see how it goes when I start the first painting this morning. Coffee ready?" he asked.

Caitlin nodded, realizing he wasn't going to go into any detail about what he had in mind. She'd just have to wait and see what transpired under his brush.

He started work as soon as the breakfast dishes had been cleared. Caitlin sensed the difference in him immediately. He was even more remote than while sketching. His face became still, his eyes half-closed behind his glasses as though he was watching something far distant. The line of concentration in his forehead seemed more deeply cut.

She responded by keeping motionless in her chair, the dog resting at her feet.

There was no talking this time. Classical music played softly in the background as Reyn stood in front of his easel, paints at hand. He examined the sketches on the drafting table, and when he looked at Caitlin it was through narrowed scrutinizing eyes. She sat quietly under the lights while he blocked in her form on the canvas.

"Tilt your head to the right," he ordered after a long period of silence. "A little more—look at me. I want to emphasize the eyes . . . that's it."

It was midafternoon when a knock on the back door interrupted them.

Caitlin smiled at the startled look on Reyn's face. He gave his head a little shake and blinked as he surfaced. Frowning, he put down his brush and went to the door, the dog at his heels.

Caitlin stretched and stood up, rubbing the back of her neck, glad for the interruption. She could hear the murmur of voices from the kitchen, then a lilting feminine laugh.

"Caitlin," Reyn said, coming back into the living room, "I'd like you to meet a friend of mine, Stevie Hayes. She does my framing. Stevie, you remember my kid sister, Gabby? This is her friend, Caitlin Carr. She's staying for a few days at Gabby's request."

That's put me in my place, Caitlin thought as she murmured a greeting.

Stevie Hayes was tall with long gold-brown hair flowing in crisp waves over a crimson waterproof cape. Wide clear gray eyes dominated an attractive face, and she held herself with graceful self-assurance.

Caitlin thought instantly of Gabby's description of Reyn's ex-wife—tall and curvy with wild blondish hair. She felt a little self-conscious as Stevie eyed her with frank appraisal.

"So this is why we haven't seen you lately." Her smile didn't quite reach her eyes.

"Caitlin's agreed to sit for me," Reyn said. "It's kept me kind of busy."

"You're doing a portrait? This I've got to see." Shrugging off her cape, she walked over to the easel and examined the canvas closely, then glanced at the sketches. "I can see it," she said thoughtfully, looking up to study Caitlin again. She nodded slowly. "It should work."

"Are you an artist, too?" Caitlin asked, feeling uncomfortable under that cool gaze.

"I sculpt—when I'm not framing for Reyn, that is. What about you?"

"I'm a teacher."

"Caitlin works with Gabby," Reyn put in. "She's on sick leave right now. Gabby thought it would do her good to get away from Vancouver for a while, and offered her the cabin. I thought she should stay here where it's more comfortable."

Stevie gave a mock shudder. "Yes, that cabin would be pretty dismal in this weather."

Caitlin gave a little nod of agreement, thinking Reyn had been quick to point out that she was Gabby's friend, not his, and that there was nothing intimate about her presence in his house.

"Can I get you some coffee, Stevie?" Reyn asked.

"Only if it comes with some of that brandy you keep around." She smiled at Reyn, her eyes crinkling attractively at the corners.

"One brandy coming up," Reyn said. "Caitlin?"

Caitlin shook her head quickly. "Actually, I'd like to go for a walk. I need to have a real stretch and a bit of exercise after all that sitting."

"It's raining, Caitlin," Reyn said. "Maybe you should wait till it stops."

Caitlin glanced out the window. "It's just a bit of mist. I won't melt," she added with a touch of sarcasm, annoyed by Reyn's paternal attitude. She wasn't going to stay, watching quietly while Reyn entertained his friend...his lover? Smiling politely at Stevie, she started toward the back entrance where she kept her jacket and shoes. "It was nice meeting you."

"You, too," Stevie answered agreeably. "Enjoy your walk."

"Don't be long," Reyn warned her. "I don't want you getting chilled."

Caitlin shot him a look of irritation over her shoulder. "I think I should be able to figure out when I've had enough."

Stevie laughed as she curled up in a corner of the couch, tucking her long legs under her. "You're sounding like a bossy big brother, Reyn. Leave the girl alone."

Caitlin grimaced as she shut the inner door, jamming her feet into running shoes. Grabbing her jacket, she went outside.

Rain fell gently, beading like dew against her skin. Taking a deep breath, Caitlin zipped up her jacket and started off toward the path to the beach. Hearing a noise, she glanced behind her. Rex was following slowly.

She grinned. "Hey Rex—want to go for a walk?" The dog's ears pricked and he watched her with bright-eyed interest. She repeated the phrase, laughing as the dog let out a yelp and bounded toward her.

"Let's go, boy," she said, glad of the company.

The beach was deserted, as it usually was on cold gray days. The tide was halfway in, the water pushing a rim of foam as it crept slowly up the sand.

Caitlin ran a bit, the dog loping ahead. A flock of gulls clustered on the rocks near the far arm of the bay. The dog spotted them, stopped his run and crouched low. Caitlin stopped to watch him.

Ears flattened and keeping well down, the dog sneaked up on the birds. All of a sudden he took off in a mad dash, and the gulls scattered. Caitlin laughed as they wheeled above her, shrieking in raucous panic.

Panting, Rex ran back to her, his rear end wriggling happily. Caitlin patted the damp fur between his ears. "Enjoyed that, did you?" She could hardly believe it, but she was overcoming her fear of Rex. He really was a gentle animal.

She continued on slowly toward the rocks. It was damp and wet, not the best of days for a long walk, but she wasn't anxious to return. In fact, she felt miserable. In spite of herself, tentative dreams had been forming, flitting through her imagination, and she'd found herself hoping that just maybe there could be something between her and Reyn.

The real world had penetrated today, shattering the quiet solitude they'd enjoyed, making her only too aware that Reyn had a life away from his easel, one he shared with beautiful women like Stevie Hayes.

IT WAS MUCH LATER when she went back to the house. Dusk seeped through the day's gray, deepening it to black. As Caitlin climbed the hill she could see the beckoning glow of light through the trees. Sighing tiredly, she crossed the yard and headed for the rear entrance. To her relief, Stevie's car was gone.

She pushed open the door, the dog nosing in ahead of her. She pulled off her wet runners and socks, then slipped out of her jacket, hanging it on a hook. She was glad to be back. The house was warm and welcoming, the air filled with the spicy scent of Italian cooking.

She blinked against the bright lights of the kitchen, smiling at Reyn as he turned from the stove. Her smile faltered when she saw his face.

Crossing his arms on his chest, he glared at her. "Where have you been?" he demanded.

Blinking in surprise, Caïtlin shrugged. "Out for a walk."

"You should have been back ages ago. Look at you—you're soaking wet. Do you want to get sick again?"

"Of course not. But I—"

"Go take a hot shower," he interrupted. "Before you get chilled."

Caitlin raised her chin defiantly, her eyes cool and distant. "I'm not a child, Reyn, to be chastised for coming home late for supper. Please don't treat me as one. I've really had enough of it." She was angry. He would never have acted this way with Stevie.

"Hey! Slow down. I'm just concerned about your health."

"Well, don't be so damned patronizing about it." She noticed with satisfaction the look of surprise on his face as she turned and stormed from the kitchen.

She took a long hot shower to warm up, knowing it was the logical thing to do, but wishing she could defy

Reyn and do without one. His bossy attitude still rankled.

After dressing in a pale pink sweater and comfortable old jeans, and pulling on a pair of fuzzy pink-and-blue striped socks, she walked slowly to the kitchen. Leaning against the doorjamb, she waited for Reyn to notice her.

He turned around and looked at her, his eyes dark and inscrutable. Suddenly he flashed a grin, then raised his hands, palms up, in a shrug. "I'm sorry, Caitlin. But you look so young."

Caitlin sighed and gave her head a little shake. It certainly wasn't the first time her diminutive stature had given someone the wrong idea about her age, but she felt particularly disappointed that Reyn couldn't see her as she really was.

"I'm twenty-five years old," she said, anger underscoring her words. "I've been on my own since I was seventeen. I may not be very big, but I'm all grown up. Kindly remember that."

"So I was worried. Don't you think you're over-reacting?"

She hated the look of amused tolerance growing on his face. "No, I don't. This has been going on since I got here and I've had enough." She glared at him. "Look at me Reyn—look!" She held up her hands and turned around slowly.

"I'm not a little girl, Reyn. I'm a woman." She ran her hands over her sides. "Physically," she said emphatically, "and mentally." She tapped a finger to her forehead. "Got it?"

He stared at her for a long moment, his surprised expression turning thoughtful. The line between his brows deepened.

"Got it?" she repeated, softer now, as she grew aware of his scrutiny.

"Got it," he said brusquely. "And you're right. I'm sorry." He crossed the room and held out his hand to her. "Friends again?"

Caitlin laid her hand in his, feeling her anger wash away. Her lashes swept down, then up again, as she met his eyes. For a moment she almost thought she'd seen something other than friendship in their depths. His fingers tightened on hers as she smiled shyly and nodded.

"Good." He pulled his hand away slowly, his thumb rubbing her palm. "Hungry?"

"Very," she said, keeping her voice light in spite of the sharp stab of feeling his touch created. "What are we having?"

"Lasagna, with salad. Go sit down and I'll bring it through."

As always, the meal was delicious. Caitlin ate with appreciation, her appetite restored.

"You know, Caitlin," Reyn began, "you didn't have to disappear this afternoon because of Stevie."

Stevie. The real world pushed in again. "I know... but I thought you might like some privacy. Did you have a nice visit?" she asked, picking up a crystal glass of ice water.

Reyn smiled and nodded. "I enjoy her company."

I'd rather not have known that. Caitlin sipped her water. She didn't want to think about Stevie, but now was the time to ask the question that had been on her mind all afternoon. "Is she your girlfriend?" she asked with candor. Lover was probably a more appropriate word, but she couldn't bring herself to use it.

Reyn chuckled. "She was once. We're just...friends now."

Caitlin nodded, remembering Gabby had told her that all Reyn's lovers seemed to become his friends once the affair was over. How many of these "friends" did he have?

"More lasagna?"

Caitlin shook her head. "No, thanks. It was great, but I've eaten too much already."

"That wasn't too much—it was barely enough. Still, it's more than you managed last week."

Caitlin shook her head at him and sighed. "You're doing it again, Reyn. Don't you think I know when I've had enough to eat?"

"You're also a lot feistier than you were last week." He grinned suddenly. "A lot!"

"I'm feeling better than I did last week. I also know you better—I figure I can talk back if you get too bossy."

"Gabby'd approve. She always accuses me of being bossy, too. Guess it's just big-brother territory." He pushed back his chair and started gathering dishes. "Let's get this cleared away."

Caitlin stood slowly and picked up her plate. He'd just made it very clear he thought of her much as he did Gabby. Just another sister, she thought, grimacing down at the scraps of food on her plate, and for a brief moment she wished she looked more like the kind of woman he was attracted to—tall and curvy with wild blondish hair.

"WOULD YOU LIKE some brandy?" Reyn asked later as Caitlin settled on the couch with a cup of coffee.

"Mmm—a bit, please. And if you promise not to frown if I add it to my coffee. That's the only way I really like it."

"It ruins the taste—but, if that's the way you want it..." He added a splash of brandy to the cup she held out for him, then sat down opposite her, cradling a snifter in his hands.

They sat in silence for a moment watching the logs in the fireplace succumb to the crackle and hiss of the flames. Rex wandered in and plopped down with a groan near Reyn's feet.

"You said you've been on your own since you were seventeen," Reyn remarked suddenly. "Did you have to move away from home to attend university?"

Caitlin took a sip of her brandy-laced coffee and nodded. "My mother was living in the Okanagan at the time, and I wanted to go to university in Vancouver."

"Did you live in the dorm?"

"No—there wasn't a lot of money." Almost none, she thought, remembering the few dollars in her possession when she'd climbed onto the bus. She glanced up and saw Reyn watching her curiously.

"I got a job as a live-in baby-sitter for a family. I looked after the kids—there were two of them—during the day while the parents worked, then went to classes at night. It didn't pay much more than spending money, but I didn't have to worry about room and board, and student loans took care of books and tuition."

"Was it very hard?"

She smiled a little and nodded. "It was at first." Home might not have been much, but it had been familiar. It had taken a lot of determination and strength not to be overwhelmed during that first year on her own.

Reyn swirled his brandy, looking at her thoughtfully. "Your parents must have been worried about you."

"There's just my mother and she . . . well, she figured I could take care of myself." Caitlin took a sip of coffee then stared down into the cup. "Actually, she was glad to see me go. Having a grown daughter made her feel old. And some of her boyfriends were starting to—" She caught herself and stopped, appalled at what she had been about to say.

"Some of the boyfriends were starting to look at you," Reyn finished quietly, nodding thoughtfully. "Where was your father?"

"My parents separated when I was three." She took another sip of coffee and forced her eyes to meet Reyn's. There was no reason not to tell him a bit about her background. "They married when they were seventeen. I was on the way and everyone seemed to think it was the right thing to do. I'm not sure that they ever really got along—I don't remember much, but I do remember the fights."

"Do you ever see your father?"

"I looked him up when I moved to Vancouver. But he's married again and has a new family. I don't see him often." It still hurt knowing that the man who had

fathered her didn't have room for her in his life, that
she had two half brothers she'd never even met.

"You're really very much alone in the world, aren't
you, Caitlin?"

"I don't feel alone. I like my life." She flashed him
a sudden grin. "I do all right."

His slow smile reflected warmly in his eyes. "I'm
sure you do, Caitlin, I'm sure you do. But isn't there
anyone you want to share your life with?"

I might consider you. The thought was as unexpected as it was clear. For a brief moment it seemed as
if she had spoken aloud and she looked away from his
watching eyes.

"Well?" he persisted softly.

"There's no one."

"Have you ever had a lover, Caitlin?"

Taken aback by the question, Caitlin's brows arched
haughtily. "That's none of your business, Reyn
Picard."

He chuckled at the expression on her face, his eyes
sparking with laughter. "I think you just answered my
question."

Caitlin looked away from him and took another sip
of her coffee. It had cooled, but the brandy gave it a
touch of warmth. She stared into the fire. "I watched
my mother make one mistake after another with men.
She was constantly falling in and out of love. She still
is."

She glanced at Reyn and shrugged. "It's made me
cautious—overly so, perhaps—but I'll wait for the
right man. I'm not going to be like her," she added
with quiet determination.

Reyn sat back in his chair, cradling his drink in his hands. His dark eyes watched her curiously. "So you've never been in love."

"No," she said with a touch of regret. "Have you?"

"Once. A long time ago."

"You were married," Caitlin stated.

Reyn frowned. "How did you—?" He stopped and answered himself. "Gabby."

Caitlin nodded. "Gabby."

His frown deepened and he ran a hand through his hair, tousling the deep waves. "Then you know all the sordid details," he said flatly.

"Gabby told me about a young man who was very much in love, and the pain he felt when his marriage ended," Caitlin said quietly. "There was nothing sordid about it."

He sighed, then raised his glass to his lips, taking a swallow of brandy. "It's not a time of my life I like to talk about."

"I don't suppose it is," Caitlin said with sympathy.

"She—Tamara—meant everything to me. I honestly thought we'd be together forever. And then one day she decided it was over, and left—with someone else."

"You were very young, weren't you?" Even now the pain he had felt was evident. She felt a pang of compassion.

"I was twenty-two when she left—married at nineteen and divorced before my twenty-third birthday. Most men are only beginning to think about settling down at that age, and I'd been through it all. It left me feeling pretty damned bitter—and cynical."

"But you outgrew those feelings."

"I suppose I did—eventually." He stared into the dying fire, old memories clouding his eyes. "But I never want to go through anything like that again. Once in a lifetime is too much."

"Does that mean you won't remarry?"

"I'm not sure," he answered slowly. "Maybe someday, but..." He looked up from the fire and frowned. "Hey—I wasn't going to talk about this."

Caitlin smiled gently at the look on his face. "I know."

"But you got me talking, anyway," he grumbled. "Must be all those psychology courses you take."

"They do come in handy," Caitlin agreed. She stood up to go to the kitchen for some more coffee, knowing it was time for a change of subject. "Can I get you anything?"

"No, thanks," he said, looking up as she passed his chair. He smiled at her, but a frown still creased his brow.

Caitlin's eyes were thoughtful as she left the room. She knew he hadn't meant to tell her as much as he had. It felt good to know he was comfortable enough with her to share a bit of what had been a very painful time for him. She didn't need to know the details. It was all too easy to understand how he must have felt.

She'd caught the fading echo of pain in Reyn's voice and knew it would be very difficult for him to lose himself in love again, to leave himself open for pain. He'd approach a relationship cautiously. He would be friendly and fun, probably a sensitive lover, but he'd guard his deeper emotions. The knowledge was disturbing. Realistically she knew she'd really never stood a chance of having him care deeply for her, but . . .

Caitlin stirred milk into her coffee and sighed. She put her spoon into the sink and turned to go back into the living room, glad she had this insight. It would enable her to keep the stirrings of attraction she felt for Reyn under control. She'd enjoy his friendship and not expect anything more.

CHAPTER FOUR

IT WAS EARLY AFTERNOON when Reyn put down his brush and pushed away from the easel. "That's enough for today," he stated.

Caitlin was surprised. He hadn't worked nearly as long as usual. Come to think of it, he'd seemed different all morning, more remote—cooler. Did he regret having opened up to her about his marriage? Was he taken aback at how much he'd revealed? Maybe he felt he had to distance himself from her, to make last night seem less personal. She hoped this mood wouldn't last. She liked his relaxed teasing manner so much more.

"Tired?" she asked, standing up to stretch.

"No, I'm going out later." He glanced at the clock on the far wall. "I want to shower and change first. You don't mind staying by yourself, do you?"

"Of course not," she said quickly, wondering where he was going.

"Good." He finished cleaning his brushes then carefully draped a cloth over the painting. "There's lots of food in the freezer—help yourself to anything you want."

"I will, thanks." Caitlin watched him leave the room, then settled down on the couch with a book on child psychology. It was a few minutes before she could concentrate on the words in front of her.

Nearly half an hour passed before Reyn returned. Caitlin put down her book, her eyes widening slightly. He was dressed in charcoal-gray woolen slacks and an expensive-looking black sweater with a dress shirt underneath.

"You look nice," she said. "Heavy date?" She hoped not.

He shrugged. "I'm taking Stevie out for dinner. I owe her one for having worked overtime on that last framing job—it was a rush order, and she really came through for me. Listen, Caitlin," he added, "there's a good chance I won't make the last ferry, so don't worry if I'm not back tonight."

"I won't," she said lightly, wondering where he would stay—as if she couldn't guess. "Enjoy yourself."

"Thanks. I will," he said, pulling on a leather jacket. Hesitating by the door, he turned around to look at her. "You're sure you'll be all right by yourself?"

Caitlin gave a sigh of exasperation. "I've stayed alone without a baby-sitter before, Reyn. Of course I'll be all right. I'm used to being on my own, remember?"

"Okay, but if you—"

"Go, Reyn. Enjoy your date. Rex and I will enjoy the peace and quiet."

Reyn chuckled as he opened the door, the dog pushing against him. "Right. See you, kid."

"Yeah—see you." Her voice was a little wistful as the door closed behind him. She got up and went to

the window, watching as he told a disappointed Rex to
stay before getting into the car. When he drove out of
sight, the dog sat back on his haunches and raised his
nose to the sky. As his low mournful howl filled the
air, Caitlin shivered and turned away from the window. The house suddenly seemed very empty.

CAITLIN COULDN'T RELAX. She tuned the radio to a
light rock station and turned up the volume, hoping to
dispel the quiet. She fed Rex and ate something herself, then tried to settle down with her books, but
couldn't concentrate.

She did a load of laundry and mopped the kitchen
floor while she waited for the clothes to dry. There was
little ironing, but she touched up Reyn's clothes and
folded them neatly before taking them to his room.

She pushed the door open and flicked on the lights,
walking slowly into his room. As she laid his clothes
on top of a dresser, she looked around.

It was an attractive room, much larger than the one
she used. There was a small brick fireplace opposite
the king-size bed. Facing the hearth were two overstuffed armchairs with a small glass-topped table in
between. Built-in shelves on each side of the fireplace
held photographs, as well as books.

Feeling a little sneaky, Caitlin examined the photos.
She was disappointed, but not surprised, to find no
picture of his ex-wife.

Most were pictures of his family. Reyn seemed as
adept with a camera as he was with a paintbrush,
Caitlin noted, smiling at the candid shots. There was
one photograph, obviously older, of a man and
woman with a young boy of about ten standing be-

tween them. The boy had dark solemn eyes, exactly like those of the woman. The man wore a slight smile and seemed relaxed, but there was a hint of sternness about him.

Reyn looked a lot like his mother. Even the expressions on their faces were similar. She'd probably died not long after the picture was taken, Caitlin thought, remembering what Gabby had told her. Reyn must have been devastated. Carefully she replaced the picture and turned to look at the rest of the room.

The bed was neatly made. A charcoal-gray comforter with a broad red stripe contrasted nicely with the light gray carpeting. Vertical blinds over sliding glass doors shut out the night and chrome-plated bedside lamps gave the room a warm glow. The air held a hint of the musky after-shave Reyn used, reminding Caitlin she had no business being in his room. Feeling as though he could somehow know, she switched off the light and left.

By ten-thirty she'd finally settled down. She sat by the fire, sipping cocoa, the dog stretched out at her feet. She looked up from her book and smiled at him, rubbing a foot gently along his rib cage, glad of his company. *Now I know why people keep dogs,* she thought.

Rex raised his head, suddenly alert, ears pricked as he looked toward the door.

Caitlin felt her heartbeat quicken and she smiled widely. Reyn was back. That meant he wasn't going to spend the night with Stevie, after all. She tried to ignore her sudden feeling of relief and satisfaction. It had been hard to keep images of the two of them together from her mind.

She heard footsteps going around to the kitchen, then a sharp knock. Startled, Caitlin sat up straight in the chair. Reyn wouldn't knock, would he? Who could it be? She glanced at the dog as the knock was repeated, but he merely lay with his muzzle on his paws, staring intently at the door.

Caitlin got up and walked cautiously to the door, thinking that a big snarling German shepherd would be nice to have right about now.

"Who is it?" she called as the knock sounded again.

The door pushed open and Gabby's grinning face appeared. "Me," she said. "I'm not disturbing anything, am I?"

Caitlin sagged with relief and scowled at her friend. "You scared me half to death, Gabby. I couldn't imagine who it could be." Rex pushed past her, tail wagging furiously as he greeted Gabby with low throaty sounds.

"Sorry." Gabby stooped to grab the dog's ruff with both hands, giving his head a little shake. "Hi ya, Rex, you goofy beast." Still grinning, she glanced at Caitlin. "Where's my bossy big brother?"

"On a date."

Gabby straightened and reached for a bulging sports bag before shutting the door. "On a date." She sighed. "Who with? No, let me guess. Megan Roth? No? Hmm—must be a new one."

"An old one, I think. Stevie Hayes."

"Oh, her." Gabby made a face as she followed Caitlin through to the living room. "I thought he was through with that one. Although she's nicer than Megan—more down to earth. Did you meet her?"

"Stevie? Yes. She dropped in yesterday."

"So, what did you think?"

Caitlin shrugged as she knelt in front of the fire to add more wood. "She seemed okay." She threw a log on the flames and replaced the screen, then sat with her back resting against the hearth. "I only talked to her for a couple of minutes."

Gabby sat down on the couch. "She didn't stay long?"

"I don't know. I went for a walk. So—what are you doing here? Where's Yvan?"

Gabby groaned. "His mother's been after him to go home for a weekend and he figured he should get it over with, especially now that we're thinking about skiing in Banff over Christmas. He wanted me to go with him, but I really can't stand her—and the feeling is obviously mutual. I told him that if we decide to get married I'll make an effort, but in the meantime I'll keep my distance. You know me, Caitlin—I get along with everyone. But she really is an old witch. How Yvan turned out so sweet I'll never know. So," she said brightening, "I decided I'd come up and see how you and my big brother are making out. Are you?"

"Am I what?"

Gabby grinned cheekily. "Making out."

Caitlin couldn't help but laugh. "He calls me kid and says I look like a little lost kitten. Believe me, Gabby, he doesn't think of me in that way at all. I'm not his type."

"Just as well. You're too sweet and innocent to handle someone like him. I wouldn't want you to get hurt." Her voice took on a serious note. "Y'know, I'm not so sure he knows what his type is. He's so busy looking for the lost love of his youth, he doesn't realize that he's endlessly dating clones of Tamara—that was his wife. He married her when he was still in university," Gabby added. "Or did I tell you that already?"

At Caitlin's nod, she continued. "Oh, well...maybe he'll come to his senses one of these days and realize that the world doesn't begin and end with tall bosomy blondes." Leaning back against the couch, she sighed deeply. "I need to unwind after that drive. What are you drinking?"

"Cocoa."

Gabby grimaced. "Let's make some coffee. I brought something to color it with—a bottle of Irish Cream."

Gabby chatted almost nonstop as she made a pot of coffee, answering Caitlin's eager questions about her class and filling her in on all the latest school gossip.

As they settled back in the living room with mugs of coffee generously laced with the creamy liqueur, Gabby sighed contentedly.

"This almost makes up for that long drive and fighting all the Friday-night traffic." She glanced at her colorful plastic wristwatch. "The last ferry just docked. Reyn should be pulling up in a few minutes."

Caitlin shook her head. "I don't think so. He told me not to expect him back tonight."

Gabby made a face. "Let me guess—he's staying at Stevie's."

"I don't know. He didn't say."

"Chances are." Gabby took a drink of coffee. "He shouldn't have left you alone like this."

"I'm *not* alone," Caitlin pointed out. "And even if I was, it wouldn't matter. Like I told him—I don't need a baby-sitter."

"Well, I still think he should be here instead of off with Stevie."

Caitlin couldn't help but agree, but she didn't say anything. She found herself glancing at the clock while Gabby chatted on. When it became obvious that Reyn wouldn't be returning that night, she felt a stab of disappointment. She took a sip of her coffee and willed herself to relax. It wasn't hard with Gabby there. Soon Caitlin was laughing over some of her friend's more outrageous comments, encouraging her with quiet remarks of her own. The evening ended much better than it had started.

GABBY GOT UP just after Caitlin the next morning, bright-eyed and perky.

"So—what do we do today?" she asked, returning from the kitchen with a cup of coffee.

Caitlin was standing by the window, enjoying the view. For the first time in a long time, the clouds had rolled away and the sun shone.

"I think we should get out and take advantage of the sunshine. It probably won't last long."

Gabby flopped down in a corner of the couch and stretched luxuriously, cupping her coffee mug in her hands. "Let's go shopping."

Caitlin turned away from the window. "Shopping on the first sunny day we've had in ages? We should go for a long walk or something."

"We can walk around the mall in Courtenay. I need a few things."

"You always need a few things. You're a compulsive shopper."

Gabby grinned. "It's people like me who keep the economy of the country from collapsing. So—want to hit the stores?"

It really didn't matter to Caitlin. "I suppose. What about Reyn?"

"We'll leave him a note if he's not here by the time we're ready to leave. And wear something a little fancy. We'll go to a nice restaurant for an early dinner. My treat."

"I packed for beachcombing—I don't have anything fancy with me. And why your treat?"

Gabby took a sip of coffee and grinned. "I've been snooping—it's your birthday next week, isn't it? Dinner will be my present to you."

"You don't have to do that," Caitlin objected.

"I know I don't have to, but I want to. C'mon, Cait—cooperate. Fall in with my plans. Life will be easier."

Caitlin sighed. "Undoubtedly. But I still don't have anything to wear."

Gabby's dark eyes sparkled with laughter. "Why do you think we're going shopping? Now, let's grab a bite to eat and get ready. There's a ferry leaving in just under an hour. Let's be on it."

GABBY'S HIGH SPIRITS made for a pleasant afternoon. It was impossible not to have fun when she was around.

Treating herself, Caitlin bought a straight black skirt of fine wool and a shimmering, dusky-rose blouse to go with it. Shoes came next, and then Caitlin used the store's dressing room to change into her new outfit. She stood for a moment looking at herself in the mirror, nodding in satisfaction. The clothes suited her, gave her an alluring air of sophistication that jeans and sweats could not. She quashed the intrusive realization that she wanted Reyn to see her this way.

"Very nice," Gabby approved as Caitlin emerged carrying her old clothes and worn runners in a shopping bag. "It's a good thing the store has a section for petites—that skirt wouldn't look the same flapping around your ankles."

"I'm not *that* short," Caitlin said, straightening the gold-clasped belt around her slim waist.

Gabby looked down at her and grinned fondly. "Yes you are. Now let's go eat."

The restaurant, in an old converted house across the river from a sawmill, served excellent food. It was an enjoyable meal, punctuated by bursts of laughter. Caitlin was glad she'd come, but found her mind wandering from time to time. Had Reyn returned home yet? How had he spent the night—merely as a guest in Stevie's home, or as her lover, locked in her arms? Disliking the direction her thoughts persisted in straying, she sighed inwardly. What Reyn did was his business. With effort, she turned her attention back to Gabrielle.

"Time to go," Gabby said later, glancing at her watch. "We should just be able to make the seven o'clock ferry. I wouldn't mind staying a bit longer, but the next one isn't until almost eight-thirty. And Reyn will be wondering what we've gotten up to." She picked up her liqueur glass and swallowed the last of her drink. "Ready?"

"Only if I can drive."

Gabby grinned and handed her the car keys. "I was counting on it," she said.

REYN GLARED AT THEM over the top of his glasses as he threw down the paper he'd been reading. "Well, it's about time you two decided to crawl home. You shouldn't have dragged Caitlin around all day like that, Gabby. You probably exhausted her."

"I'm fine," Caitlin put in quickly. Between Reyn and Gabby, she'd had about all the concern she could take. "If I'd felt tired, I would have said something."

"Yeah, Reyn," Gabby said cheerfully. "You should have been with us, anyway, but you lingered too long over coffee and croissants at what's-her-name's this morning." She kicked off her shoes and flopped down on the couch. "I thought you'd broken up with her."

"Stevie and I are still business associates, as well as good friends. She wanted my advice about something."

Gabby wrinkled her nose in disapproval. "This advice took all night?"

Frowning, Reyn removed his glasses and laid them on the table beside him. "Gabby—"

Gabby sighed and raised her hands. "I know, I know. It's none of my business."

"See if you can remember that for once," Reyn said firmly. He turned to Caitlin as she sat patting the dog, listening to their exchange. "How was dinner?"

"Very nice," she answered with a quick smile, her hair swinging against her cheek as she glanced up at him. He was looking at her closely, his frown line deepening as he took in her changed appearance.

What was the matter? Didn't he like the way she looked?

"It was her birthday present from me," Gabby volunteered.

"Oh? When's your birthday?" Reyn asked Caitlin, his frown softening.

"Friday," Gabby answered for her. "You'll have to bake her a cake, Reyn. Is there any coffee made?" she demanded, changing the subject. "Or do I have to make it myself?"

"Make it yourself," Reyn said mildly. "And while you're at it, make enough for me, too. I wouldn't mind a cup."

"Some host," Gabby grumbled as she got up and headed for the kitchen. "I suppose you want some of my Irish Cream, too," she threw over her shoulder.

Reyn shook his head. "I'll have some brandy. What would you like, Caitlin?"

"Just coffee, thanks," she said. She was curled up in an armchair, head tilted to one side, her eyes twinkling. She enjoyed seeing Reyn and Gabby together. Under all the banter was obvious affection.

"You're staring," she accused him after a moment of silence. It didn't really bother her. She'd become used to him watching her.

"Sorry." He smiled at her lazily, his eyes lingering on her face. "It's just...you look very pretty tonight, Caitlin. That blouse brings out your coloring. Your skin is a creamy satin, your eyes...luminous. I haven't seen you quite like this before. You look..."

"Grown-up?" she supplied dryly, but inside she felt a flutter of pleasure. He made her sound sexy.

He laughed, but then seemed distant as a frown swept away his smile. He looked from her face to the delicate swell of her breasts and the curve of her hips. "Very grown-up," he admitted, and his frown deepened as he turned to watch the flames.

Caitlin cautioned herself not to take his words seriously. He had the same look about him just now as he had when standing in front of his easel. She told herself that he wasn't really seeing her as much as he was thinking about applying paint to the canvas. Still, her heartbeat quickened. Tonight he'd finally seen her as a woman. It might not mean much, but she couldn't prevent herself from fantasizing just a little.

IT WAS LATE when Gabby announced that she was going to bed.

"And so you should," Reyn agreed. "You're half-sloshed."

"You're just sore because I won that last poker hand...and because Caitlin won most of the rest." She grinned cheekily at her brother. "You're a poor loser, Reyn Picard."

"Am not."

"Are too."

Caitlin held up a hand in protest. "Stop it," she demanded, her eyes alight with laughter. "I've had about all the sibling rivalry I can take for one night."

"And all the nickels," Reyn grumbled. "We really should have a few more hands. I'm sure it was just beginner's luck. It should be wearing off any minute now."

"We'll get her next time." Gabby smothered a yawn with the back of her hand. She pushed back her chair, stumbling a bit as she stood up.

"What'd I tell you?" Reyn said to Caitlin. "Half-sloshed." He stood up and offered an arm to Gabby. "C'mon, kid. I'll make sure you get home safely."

Caitlin followed them down the hallway to the bedrooms, laughing at Gabby's exaggerated sway as Reyn tried to stop her from walking into the walls. *They really do like to ham it up,* she thought. They'd joked and laughed throughout the evening. Caitlin was a little surprised at how easily Reyn had gone along with Gabby, no matter how outrageous she'd become. She'd thought he would be more standoffish, more reserved. This was a new side of him she enjoyed seeing.

"Go sleep it off," Reyn ordered Gabby as he opened her bedroom door and pushed her in.

"You're bossy, Reyn," Gabby complained, making a face.

"And you're a brat," Reyn returned mildly. "Do you drink this much all the time?"

Gabby clutched the door and grinned. "Only when I'm around you." She tilted her head to the side and tapped one of her soft round cheeks with the tip of her finger. "Night, Reyn."

Reyn bent and dutifully kissed her cheek. "Night, brat."

"Night, Caitlin," Gabby called over her shoulder.

"Good night, Gabby." Caitlin smiled as Gabby shut the door, then she made her way down the hall. Reyn followed.

Caitlin stopped at her own room, one hand on the doorknob. She turned to see Reyn behind her, and she smiled tentatively, her breathing becoming shallow as he stepped closer. She could see a questioning look in his velvety eyes and prayed he couldn't see just how attracted to him she was.

"Good night, Reyn," she said softly, wanting to disappear into the safety of her room.

Reyn looked down at her and smiled lazily. "Don't I get to kiss you good-night, too?"

Caitlin felt her pulse throb erratically, but her expression didn't change. Coolly she raised her head and tilted it to one side.

Reyn curled a finger under her chin and turned her to face him. "Good-night kisses on the cheek are for sisters," he murmured, "and you're not that, are you?" He leaned down to brush her lips with his.

It was meant to be a light touch, Caitlin knew, a teasing caress. But her lips clung instinctively to his warm soft mouth, and as she kissed him, a tingling spark of awareness grew deep within.

She drew away, catching the flash of surprise in Reyn's eyes as he raised his head and stepped back. She felt a fleeting sense of satisfaction, and smiled with hard-won composure as she opened the door to her room. "Good night, Reyn," she said quietly.

Reyn jammed his hands in the pockets of his jeans and stared at her with narrowed eyes. "Good night, Caitlin," he echoed as she went into her room and closed the door behind her.

She leaned against the door, her bottom lip caught between her teeth as she listened to his retreating footsteps. That kiss had started—and ended—innocently enough, but it had awakened a spark of desire.

And Reyn? Sighing a little, she began to undress. Reyn had been surprised—she had seen that plainly enough—but what caused his surprise she couldn't tell. Was he simply taken aback by the fact that she'd kissed him, or had he felt the same spark?

Caitlin pulled on her pajamas and crawled into bed, reaching over to turn out the lamp. As she settled down and pulled the covers snug around her, she again saw the look of surprise in Reyn's eyes.

What if that little kiss had aroused something in him? What would she do if after tonight he saw her in a different light, not just as Gabby's friend? Or nice enough but not really his type? Caitlin frowned into the darkness, thinking about what an affair with Reyn might mean.

Physically it would be very satisfying. Without being quite sure how she knew, Caitlin had no doubt that Reyn would be a wonderful lover. He was sensitive and kind and had an appealing sense of humor. She couldn't pick a better man—if all she wanted was a lover.

She wanted more. She needed more.

If having an affair with Reyn ever became an option, she would have to acknowledge one thing. He wasn't in love with her. Nor was he likely ever to be.

Tonight she sensed something had changed. But did she really want that change? She liked knowing Reyn was her friend. Friendships lasted. If Reyn became her lover, she would lose that friendship when the affair came to an end. And it would end, she knew. It would dwindle to the occasional weekend after she left the island and returned to the real world.

If that happened—no, *when* that happened—she'd lose Reyn completely. Because she couldn't see herself reverting to mere friendship after he had been her lover. It would kill her to see another woman in his life, sharing the intimacy that had once been hers.

It would be best to let the spark of desire flicker out. Reyn wasn't going to offer her the firm rock of commitment she needed. And no matter how she felt about Reyn, without commitment, there would be nothing.

She needed permanence. She needed a future.

CHAPTER FIVE

CAITLIN WAS SITTING in the living room looking out at the day when Gabby came in.

"Morning," her friend said, blinking sleepily.

"Morning. Coffee's ready."

"Great. I could use about a gallon." Yawning, Gabby trudged into the kitchen, her fuzzy purple slippers slapping against the floor.

Caitlin smiled as Gabby returned, clutching a mug of coffee. "Feeling all right?"

Gabby huddled in a corner of the couch, tucking her pink housecoat under her legs. "I'll be fine as soon as the coffee kicks in." She smothered a yawn, then ran a hand through her short brown hair, causing it to stick up in little spikes. "Been awake long?"

"Not long. I was thinking I should go for a walk— it looks like another nice day—but I can't seem to get going. Maybe later." Caitlin took a sip of coffee, then put the mug on the table beside her. "When are you leaving?"

"I'll catch the twelve-thirty ferry. I don't want to get home after dark. How about you, Cait? How much longer are you going to stay here?"

"I'm not sure—it depends when Reyn finishes the painting."

"Painting? What painting?"

Caitlin looked at her in surprise. "Don't you know? Reyn's doing a painting of me. That's why I've stayed here so long."

Gabby put her mug down and got up to go over to the easel. She flipped off the cover and stood looking at the painting. "So *that's* how he got you to stay," she said, glancing thoughtfully at Caitlin.

"What do you mean?"

"When he told me how sick you were, I explained that if he valued his own health he'd better take care of you, and that a few extra days here would probably do you a world of good." She grinned. "He warned me you were a stubborn little thing and that he couldn't see how he was going to stop you from leaving short of tying you to the bed."

Caitlin frowned. "And?"

"I told him he should be smart enough to think of something a little less kinky, and that I didn't want to see you back in Vancouver before the end of the week." She looked at the painting again. "I thought he'd just managed to convince you that a few days here would give you a chance to recuperate. I should have figured you wouldn't give in that easily."

Caitlin strained to keep her face impassive. Oh, she'd always known that it had been Gabby's concern over her health that prompted Reyn to take her in. But she hadn't realized Gabby had coerced him into making sure she stayed put for a while. He'd made her believe she *owed* him for interrupting his work, that sitting for him was the payment he *wanted*.

But he didn't really want to paint her, Caitlin thought hollowly. It was just a ploy to get her to stay. Something to appease Gabby. She'd been flattered that a respected artist like Reyn was interested in having her pose for him. She might have known it wasn't for real.

"It's a good painting," Gabby conceded. "The boy has talent. Have you seen it yet?"

Caitlin shook her head. "No. I thought I'd wait until it was finished." Which meant she'd never see it.

"Cait? Is something wrong?"

Caitlin looked up to see the concern in Gabby's eyes. She forced a smile. "I'm still a bit sleepy, I guess."

"You *are* feeling okay, aren't you? You look so much better than you did last time I saw you, I hardly thought to ask."

"I feel fine, thanks. All I needed was a good rest, and I've had that. I think maybe I'll head home soon." Soon, as in later today. After she had it out with Reyn. She'd let him know exactly how his pretense made her feel.

"There's no rush. From what I've seen, Reyn's gotten kind of used to your being around. It's good for him, I'm sure." Gabby stood up and stretched, then picked up her mug and headed for the kitchen. "Let's get some breakfast. If we wait for that brother of mine, we'll starve to death."

GABBY LEFT shortly after noon to catch the ferry to Vancouver Island. Caitlin watched her go, wishing she was leaving with her. She felt down. Nothing was as it had seemed.

"Ah, peace and quiet," Reyn sighed as Gabby drove out of sight.

"Gabby's fun," Caitlin stated firmly, turning away from the window.

"But exuberant. And talkative. I prefer the quiet type." He smiled. "Like you."

Caitlin said nothing. She walked over to the fire and knelt beside the hearth where the dog lay sleeping. She rubbed his ears as she gazed into the flames. It was completely different being here now. For a while she'd felt as though she belonged, as though Reyn was a friend. Now she knew he'd simply come up with a novel way of ensuring she stayed in order to keep Gabby off his back.

Reyn came to stand by the fireplace, hands in the pockets of his jeans as he looked down at her. "Caitlin, is something wrong? You seem—distant."

Caitlin traced a finger along the edge of the dog's white mask and said nothing. It was hard to put what she was feeling into words.

"Is it . . ." He was frowning as he sat on the edge of the hearth. "Are you upset because I kissed you last night?"

Caitlin glanced at him and shook her head quickly. In the course of this morning's revelations she'd all but forgotten about it. "Of course not."

"Are you sure?"

"Oh, Reyn—of course I am. It was just a little good-night kiss between friends." Put in perspective, that's all it was.

"Then it's something else." He leaned toward her, arms resting on his thighs.

Caitlin looked back at the dog, her hair swinging against her cheek, hiding her face from Reyn. She was usually quite adept at hiding her feelings, but this mixture of anger and hurt was hard to keep inside.

"Tell me, Caitlin" he demanded.

Caitlin caught her bottom lip between her teeth and frowned. "I feel a little foolish," she said finally.

"Foolish?" he echoed. "Why?"

She tilted her head toward him. "I thought you really wanted to paint me. Now I realize it was the only way you could think of to keep me here, to satisfy Gabby. You should have known she was overreacting. I was quite capable of going home once my cold was over."

Her anger warred with disappointment, and she jumped up to face him, hands on her hips. "Dammit, Reyn. Why did you do it?"

"Do what?"

She threw up her hands in exasperation. "Pretend! I mean, I couldn't figure out why you would want to paint me, but I at least thought you were sincere." She turned away from him. "I'm catching the next ferry."

"You can't—the painting isn't finished yet. And I've got another one I want to do."

Eyes flashing, Caitlin turned back to look at him. "Give it up, Reyn. I'm on to you now, remember? No more pretense."

"Calm down and listen to me," Reyn demanded. "Gabby did ask me to let you stay for a few days longer, but I certainly didn't start that painting just to keep you here. Don't you realize by now that I take my work very seriously? And there was something about you . . . I wanted to paint you, Caitlin." He stood up abruptly. "Come and take a look at it."

Slowly Caitlin followed him over to the easel. She crossed her arms tightly over her chest as she stood to one side.

Reyn folded back the draped cloth and stepped away. "Look at it, Caitlin. There's no pretense."

And there she was—crouched beside the dog, one hand resting on his head. *Reyn was right about the coloring,* she marveled. Her face was pale and creamy, the dog's mask a soft white, his surrounding fur the same reddish hue as her hair. Eyes of identical pale ice-blue captured attention.

They were wary eyes, cautious and not quite trusting.

Caitlin stared at the painting for a long moment, feeling her anger seep away. Did he really see her like that? Not just wary and cautious, but... He had made her beautiful. Desirable, even. She remembered the tingling spark of awareness when his lips had brushed hers and wondered if just maybe he found her attractive, after all.

"Well?"

She calmed the rush of hope she felt and turned to him. "I see you stuck to the wildlife theme—I look like a frightened rabbit." But it was good. Very good.

Reyn's brown eyes crinkled at the corners as he grinned. "That's what you looked like the first time I saw you—scared of Rex and wielding that piece of wood in your hand. And Rex looks like that whenever someone new comes around. He's never really gotten over his fear of people."

"Do you think I'm afraid of people, too?"

"Not afraid—cautious. You don't trust easily, do you, Caitlin?"

She gave a noncommittal shrug and examined the painting again. It came as no real surprise that Reyn had managed to see below the surface.

He was watching her closely. "What about me, Caitlin? Do you trust me?"

She gazed at him for a long moment, then smiled, glad that she could again. "I wouldn't still be here if I didn't."

"So you'll stay?"

"Do you really want me to?"

His answering smile was slow and warm. "I wouldn't ask if I didn't."

As his eyes held hers, she remembered how dark they'd seemed after that brief kiss at the bedroom door. A rush of desire warmed her and she glanced quickly away, surprised at how much she wanted him to kiss her again...and again. She went to stand by the window, looking out onto the bright sunlit yard.

"I—I guess I can stay a little longer," she agreed hesitantly, temptation overriding a tiny voice of caution.

"Good. Then what do you say to a picnic on the beach? We can't stay inside on a day like this."

Caitlin took a slow deep breath and turned away from the window. "That sounds like fun," she said, and managed a smile.

THERE WERE OTHERS on the beach, enjoying the Sunday sunshine. Reyn raised his hand in greeting to those he knew, but kept walking, a backpack of sandwiches and drinks slung over one shoulder, binoculars over the other. Caitlin lengthened her stride to keep up with him as they headed for the far arm of the bay. Rex roamed on ahead, disappearing from sight as his nose caught some elusive scent.

It was a perfect day. Sunlight glinted on rolling waves, dazzling the eye. It caught the green of tree-tops towering against the blue sky and brought distant mainland mountains into sharp relief. The sand above the high-tide mark was a pale gray while retreating waters left a widening strip of a darker shade patterned with clusters of brown and green seaweed.

Seals sunned themselves on black water-worn rocks just offshore. Reyn stopped when they reached the edge of the bay and gazed out at them. Dropping the pack to the ground, he took the binoculars and focused them on the seals. Then he squatted, reached for the pack and took out a sketch pad and pencil. With obvious second thoughts, he turned to Caitlin, pad in hand.

"Do you mind?" he asked. "I like the lighting—the rays are low and long, front-lighting the seals and rocks. And the waves are kind of rolling—oily-looking."

"Haven't you seen it a thousand times?" she teased.

He gave her a quick grin. "Ah, but never quite like this. Do you mind?" he asked again.

Caitlin waved a hand. "Go for it. I'll be happy to sit here with the sun on my back." She smiled to herself as he turned away, raising the binoculars to his eyes again.

Caitlin settled herself comfortably on the sand and watched Reyn. He was oblivious to anything but transferring the scene in front of him to the sketch pad propped against his knees. She enjoyed watching him, appreciated the intensity of his concentration—even felt a twinge of envy for his talent. It must be immensely satisfying.

She leaned back and raised her head, letting her eyes sweep the sky, following the flight of a lone raven until it disappeared among the trees. The sun wasn't strong, but it felt good. She felt good.

A smile played across her face as she picked up a broken piece of shell lodged between a couple of rocks. She ran a finger over its smooth surface, thinking how glad she was to be staying. In less than two weeks she would have to return to Vancouver and her job, but in the meantime, she'd savor every moment she had left on the island—with Reyn. It had been awful to think he'd only asked her to stay as a favor to Gabrielle, that the whole painting thing was a sham. But now...

Her smile deepened as she traced the worn edge of the shell. It felt wonderful knowing Reyn really wanted her to stay. She turned to look at him only to discover he was no longer facing the ocean. His lean sure fingers moved swiftly over the page, and this time it was her image that appeared. He glanced up and grinned.

"You looked lost in happy thoughts," he said. "What were you thinking?"

"Oh, just how nice it is to be here." *With you,* she added silently. "It's such a change from the city. I'm beginning to realize I don't get away enough."

"Too few do. They should—cities insulate people from nature." He frowned. "Makes it easy for them to ignore things like pollution, endangered wildlife. If we don't all wake up soon, it'll be too late to stop this downward spiral we're on. We have to realize the planet doesn't have an infinite supply of resources and start acting accordingly."

Another sudden grin chased away his frown. "I'll save the rest of the lecture for the unconverted." He flipped the sketch pad closed and returned it to the pack.

"Let's get a fire going and eat. I'm hungry."

Caitlin stood up, brushing sand from her jeans. "So am I." But her thoughts were wantonly straying. A new and very different hunger was growing in her.

"Good. I nuked some sausages—all we have to do is brown them over the fire. And I brought rolls and butter and Dijon mustard."

Caitlin looked at him with raised eyebrows. "Nuked? That sounds pretty heavy coming from a confirmed conservationist."

"Microwaved then," he explained with a laugh. "They take too long to cook otherwise. Let's set up over there." He pointed back toward the sandy bay. "I see some beached logs we can use for seats. You start gathering driftwood and I'll find a couple of branches for roasting the sausages."

In no time they had a fire burning brightly. The dog, having finished his run, came and flopped down between them, panting softly as he watched Reyn take food from the backpack. Along the beach, people began packing up and leaving as the afternoon drew to an end.

Reyn handed Caitlin a canned soft drink, his fingers brushing against hers. She thanked him, wondering if he, too, had felt a tingle of awareness.

"Do you want to eat now?" he asked.

The thoughts and feelings pinging through her mind left her with little appetite for food. She took a sip of her drink, taking a moment to pull herself together, then shook her head.

"The flames are still too high. I'll wait for the coals. I don't suppose you brought any marshmallows for dessert, did you?"

Reyn fished around in the pack and held up a bag with a grin. "Of course I did. I keep some on hand just for occasions like this—and for cups of cocoa on those long cold winter nights."

"Mmm—I can hardly wait. Marshmallows always were my favorite part of a wiener roast." She shared a warm smile with him as she settled back against a half-buried silvery log. After that awful start, it had become a perfect day.

They sat in companionable silence until the sun was almost gone, hidden by the trees behind them. Long shadows splayed over the sand to touch the water creeping inward. Gold touched the snow-capped mainland mountains and Mars rose in the eastern sky, a spark of red against a wash of fading blue. The beach was deserted, the ocean a peaceful background murmur.

Caitlin watched Reyn lay out the sausages and rolls on a blue-rimmed white enamel plate, which he put on a log near the fire. He added a small plastic bowl of butter and a jar of mustard, then laid a couple of knives on the plate.

"It's ready when you are," he said, breaking off a piece of sausage and tossing it to the dog.

"Then I guess I'd better eat before Rex gets it all." She picked up a sharpened stick and reached for a sausage, impaling it lengthwise on the point. Finding a place where the flames had died to glowing coals, she started cooking the meat.

"I'll get your bun ready. How do you want it?"

"Lots of butter, just a little mustard, please." She rotated her stick as the sausage began to sizzle and spit onto the coals. "It smells great," she said after a moment. "I'm hungrier than I thought."

"So am I." Reyn handed her a bun on a paper napkin.

"Thanks." She wrapped the bun around the sausage and took a bite. It was hot and spicy, and tasted wonderful.

Reyn leaned back. "Now, this is—" He stopped abruptly and raised his head, listening. There was a crashing in the underbrush behind them, and the sudden sharp bark of a dog. Reyn reached out and grabbed the chain collar around Rex's neck as the husky sat up, ears pricked and muscles tensed.

"Stay, Rex. Good boy," Reyn murmured, narrowing his eyes as he stared into the deepening dusk.

"What is it?" Caitlin asked, sitting upright and following Reyn's gaze.

There was another bark, followed instantly by a higher-pitched yelping howl. A deer rushed out of the brush just feet from where they sat, stumbled, then ran on toward the water.

Cursing, Reyn was on his feet. "Hold Rex," he ordered her and reached for a piece of driftwood.

Caitlin scrambled to grab the dog's chain, gripping it tightly in her fist as Rex tugged, resisting her hold. She could feel his tension.

'The deer stood on splayed legs just offshore. Its head hung low, its muzzle scant inches from the foamy wavelets, mouth gaping in a frantic attempt to draw oxygen.

Four, then five dogs tore out from the bush in hot pursuit, feral with bloodlust.

Reyn shouted and brandished the piece of driftwood like a club. The dogs skidded to a stop. Heads slinking warily, they watched Reyn.

"Home!" he shouted, hitting the sand with the wood. "Go home!" He moved toward them, shouting again.

His commanding presence overrode instinct. Three of the dogs turned and disappeared into the bush. Two backed off a bit, but remained on the sand, wary of Reyn, but unafraid. As he moved toward them again, they slunk out of sight.

Sensing the danger was gone, the deer succumbed to exhaustion, her legs slowly giving way. She collapsed onto her knees, then onto her side. As they watched, the doe laid her head on the sand, her flared nostrils barely clearing the water.

"Reyn, what can we do?" Caitlin asked softly, distressed beyond measure.

Reyn's voice was grim. "Not much, other than making sure those dogs don't return. The doe's totally exhausted. They must have been after her for quite a while." He came back to the fire and knelt beside Rex, rubbing the dog's ears. Rex swiped at his master's hand with his tongue, then looked off into the night, still alert.

"I'm going to stay down here until she's strong enough to get away. I'm not so sure those last two dogs

have gone very far—they had that look about them."
His gaze returned to the water and the deer, motionless except for the rapid rise and fall of her rib cage.

"Will she be all right?" Caitlin asked, her eyes wide with worry.

"I don't know. It's hard to say—the exhaustion, combined with intense fear..." He shrugged. "We'll just have to wait and see."

"Do we frighten her?"

"I doubt it at this point, not as long as we keep our distance and don't startle her. I think we should get Rex out of here, though."

"I'll take him up to the house."

"That's probably a good idea. You don't mind? It'll be dark soon."

Caitlin shook her head. "I don't mind. Will he come with me, or should I keep a hold on his collar?"

"He might be tempted to go off after those dogs. Just a sec—" Reyn pulled the drawstring cord from the waist of his jacket. "Here, let me loop this through his collar... There, that should make things easier."

Caitlin took the cord from Reyn and tugged on it gently. "Let's go, Rex."

"Thanks, Caitlin," Reyn called softly as she led Rex away. "Don't wait up. I could be down here for most of the night."

Caitlin waved, then headed down the shore in the deepening dusk, Rex trotting at her side.

Darkness set in before she got back to the house. She picked her way slowly over the last few yards, careful not to come down wrong on the uneven ground. A sprained ankle was the last thing she needed.

Once inside, she untied Rex, then started some coffee brewing. Reyn had seemed to think she would stay up at the house while he kept watch over the deer on the beach. He was wrong.

She found a thermos in one of the cupboards. Before filling it with coffee, she added some of Reyn's brandy. It might not be the way he liked to drink it, but she was sure he'd welcome it before the night was through. There was a flashlight in a kitchen drawer. She took that, as well as a blanket, and started back down to the beach.

As she began to slowly descend the path, flashlight beam bobbing before her, she could hear Rex's low mournful howl protesting his confinement to the house.

A half-moon clung to the velvety indigo sky. When Caitlin reached the sand, she switched off the flashlight, giving her eyes a moment to adjust to the moonlight before she started off again. Far down the beach she could see the spark of Reyn's fire. She fought back a niggling trickle of fear that the dogs might be lurking somewhere nearby, watching her, and started walking.

As she approached, she could begin to make out Reyn's form outlined by the fire. The deer still lay where she had dropped, a dark shape on the sand, her muzzle lying just clear of the water.

Caitlin stopped before Reyn became aware of her presence and watched him. He sat by the fire, resting his back against one of the logs. His knees were up, his sketch pad resting across them. Caitlin smiled, wondering what image was forming under the swift movements of his hand. She took a step forward, then stopped again, as his head came up and he looked toward the deer. Firelight flickered across the lean planes of his face.

It came to Caitlin then, not with thunderbolts and lightning, but rather with a quiet warming glow and little surprise. She was in love with him.

She stood just beyond the perimeter of firelight overwhelmed with new fears and new emotions. It was inevitable, she supposed, and more than a little disconcerting. Would he see it in her face, sense it from her actions? And if he did, what would it mean to him? He would be mildly embarrassed, she realized, perhaps pitying. And kind, gently trying to ensure she didn't get hurt. She clutched the blanket she was carrying tightly and sighed into the night.

Conditioned by a childhood of loneliness and disappointments, she didn't consider for a moment he might return her love. He liked her well enough, she knew, but his interest in her seemed to lie mainly in painting her. It amused him to do portraiture after years of concentrating on wildlife; perhaps the change challenged him.

She'd be a fool to think there would ever be any more to their relationship than there was already. Her lips moved in a wry little smile. She might have fallen in love with him, but she could still see clearly. Even if things did change, the most he would offer would be an affair—and when it was over, friendship.

A night breeze stirred cool damp air against her flushed cheeks and she shivered a little. She'd been over all this before. To take Reyn as a lover would be to lose him from her life. Once she gave him her love, she could never return to friendship. It would have to be all—or nothing.

Closing her eyes briefly, she took a deep breath, willing her emotions deep inside, away from Reyn's dark penetrating eyes. She squared her shoulders and smiled, then stepped into the rim of firelight.

Startled from his concentration, Reyn looked up. "I didn't expect to see you back." He put the sketch pad to one side and stretched.

Caitlin knelt, unwrapping the blanket from around the thermos. "I thought you might need these." She removed the plastic cup from the thermos and poured some of the brandy-laced coffee into it. "How's the deer?"

Reyn smiled his thanks as he took the steaming cup from her hands. "It's hard to say. She's still alive, and alert enough from what I can tell. I got as close as I dared without scaring her further—I can't see any cuts. With any luck all she needs is rest."

He took a swallow of coffee, then grinned at her. "Perfect," he said. "Sometimes this is definitely the best way to drink brandy."

"It's the only way," Caitlin assured him. She poked at the fire with one of the roasting sticks, not wanting to look at him directly, unsure that she'd managed to hide her feelings. "Are the dogs gone?" she asked.

"I've heard some rustling in the bush, but I couldn't see anything. I'll take a look with the flashlight in a few minutes." He handed her the plastic cup. "Here—have some."

"Thanks," Caitlin murmured, again aware of the brush of his fingers as she took the cup from him. For a moment she allowed herself to imagine how it would feel to have those hands caressing her with love and longing. She drank slowly, staring into the fire as she strove to squelch the flames dancing inside.

"You're worried about the doe, aren't you?" Reyn asked, watching her face.

Caitlin looked at him and nodded. If he thought her preoccupation was solely because of the deer, so much the better. "Does it happen often?"

"Often enough. Most dogs wouldn't give much more than a token chase, but in others the instinct to kill is strong, especially when they pack with other dogs. Owners just don't see it. If they did, they wouldn't be as inclined to let them run free." He took back the cup she offered, draining it before standing up.

"I'll go check things out," he said, picking up the flashlight.

Caitlin watched the beam of light bob before him as he melded into the night. She took a piece of driftwood from the pile they'd gathered earlier and threw it onto the fire. A dusting of cherry sparks spiraled into the sky, becoming lost in the sprinkle of stars.

Reyn shouted suddenly, jarring the quiet night. Startled, Caitlin jumped up, looking inland, but was unable to see anything but a brief flash of light. Turning, she walked slowly toward the deer. As her eyes adjusted to the dimness, she could see that the animal was now lying in a more natural position, her legs folded against her side and her head up. Not wanting to scare her further, Caitlin moved back to the fire.

As she sat, she picked up Reyn's sketch pad from on top of his pack. It was open to the drawing he'd been working on when she'd come back.

He'd sketched a stag held at bay by a pack of dogs, antlered head sagging with exhaustion as it stood facing its pursuers. Half-finished as it was, Caitlin could see the feral gleam in the dogs' eyes and sense the stag had met its end. She shuddered a bit, then flipped the page. This time her own image met her eyes.

He had drawn her sitting cross-legged in the sand, her eyes and smile dreamy as she gazed off into the distance. He'd made her look soft and vulnerable, caught up in dreams. She studied it carefully. She liked the way he made her look.

The seals on the next page blended with the smooth rocks as they basked in the sun, but their eyes glistened with awareness and the promise of action at any moment. It never ceased to amaze her, his ability to convey so much with so few strokes of a pencil.

Looking up, she saw the beam of the flashlight through the trees. Putting the sketch pad back where she'd found it, she settled against a log and waited for Reyn to return.

"They were still there," he said, coming into the firelight. "Two of them, anyway—the black-and-white mongrel and the one that looked like a shepherd. They ran off when I shouted, but I wouldn't be surprised if they didn't go far." He switched off the flashlight and dropped lithely onto the sand across from Caitlin.

"So we're staying?" she asked.

"I will. You can go back to the house if you want."

"I'd like to stay. If you don't mind." She poked at the fire again, not looking at him directly.

"I don't mind at all." He inclined his head toward the deer. "Did she react when I shouted?"

Caitlin nodded. "She's up on her side now, with her head off the sand."

"Good. She'll probably be on her feet before morning. Are you sure you want to stay? It's going to get a lot colder and damper before this is over."

"We've got a fire, hot coffee—with brandy yet— and a blanket. There's even food left over from our picnic." She looked up suddenly and grinned. "Why would I want to give this up just for a hot bath and warm bed?"

Reyn returned her grin, his eyes crinkling at the corners. "My feelings exactly. And speaking of coffee, would you like some more?"

She nodded. "Yes, please."

He poured another cupful, took a sip of it and handed it to her. "I don't know about you, but I'm getting hungry. I didn't get more than a couple of bites of my sausage—I think it hit the sand when I jumped up after those dogs."

Caitlin nibbled on a roll while Reyn roasted another sausage over the fire, sharing the coffee with him. She didn't feel hungry at all. There were too many butterflies in her stomach, she admitted ruefully.

Reyn was talking quietly between bites of food, telling her about his experiences on the Queen Charlotte Islands during a previous winter and how he'd joined with the Haida Indians to protest logging on ancestral lands. Caitlin listened sympathetically and made appropriate comments, but her thoughts kept straying.

She was in love. With Reyn. Exhilaration warred with dismay. Tingling emotion was dampened by common sense. Part of her wanted to dance with joy. Logic kept her sober. Loving someone did not ensure being loved in return.

Reyn had given no sign he regarded her with other than an almost brotherly affection—gentler, perhaps, than that he gave Gabby, but along the same lines. *But he painted me as desirable,* she insisted, hope winning out momentarily. Her spirits sank. Even that meant little if he couldn't love her the way she yearned to be loved—and she didn't think he could.

"Caitlin? You're quiet. What are you thinking?"

Years of practice came to her aid. Taking a slow deep breath, she buried her feelings and was able to meet Reyn's eyes without revealing her thoughts. Her lips formed a smile and she shook her head. "Not much," she said lightly. "The fire is so mesmerizing." She took another deep breath, more audible this time and gazed out into the night. "It's so beautiful. Peaceful."

"It is, isn't it," Reyn agreed, but he was looking at her, his eyes narrowed as they lingered on her face. He reached suddenly for his sketch pad and pencil.

Caitlin groaned as he began to fill yet another page with her image. "Again? I would have thought you'd be thoroughly bored with me by now."

Firelight flickered across his face as he looked up and shook his head. "Never. I'm fascinated by the subtle play of emotion I see on your face. You aren't nearly as closed as I thought at first."

Her heart tripped an anxious beat. "Are you saying you can read me like a book?"

He smiled slowly and shook his head again. "Only the cover, Caitlin. You don't let anyone see what's really inside, do you?"

Caitlin gave a noncommittal shrug. Picking up her stick, she poked at the fire. "And you do?"

"Sometimes I feel my paintings lay all my emotions out for everyone to see."

"But only how you feel about our endangering of the planet—wildlife. Not your personal self. You hide that as much as anyone does."

He smiled in agreement. "I suppose I do. It makes us less vulnerable, doesn't it?"

Caitlin looked up and nodded. "Less easy to hurt," she said softly.

"Has life hurt you, Caitlin?"

She was slow to answer. "Not hurt. Not really. Not when I think about what's been done to some of my kids." She jabbed at the fire, her eyes following the flight of sparks. "Disappointed might be a better word." She lowered her eyes from the dark sky and glanced at him. "What about you?" she asked quietly.

He was thoughtful for a moment, tapping his pencil against the edge of the sketch pad. "I was hurt," he admitted finally. "First by my mother's death, then by my father's obvious disapproval when I persisted with my painting instead of turning to sports or whatever his idea of a real man's course of life should be." Reyn's lips tightened in memory. "And then later there was Tamara." He stood up abruptly, as though sorry he'd said so much.

"Let's walk down the beach a bit." He closed his sketch pad and tucked it into the backpack.

"What about the deer? What if the dogs come back?"

"We won't go far," he assured her. "And I think they've probably got the message by now. Coming?"

Caitlin scrambled to her feet. Brushing damp sand from her jeans, she followed him into the night.

The deer hadn't moved much. She still lay on the sand, but her head swiveled to watch them as they walked quietly past.

The moon hung above the strait. Silver light trailed across rippled water and caught on wispy strands of mist hovering over the sand. The night had a soft eerie glow.

When Reyn held out his hand, Caitlin took it without hesitation, welcoming his warm touch on her cold fingers. It made him seem close and caring to her.

They walked slowly, near the water's edge. Just offshore, a gentle roll of waves sparked with luminous moonlight before washing quietly over the sand.

Reyn stopped and turned to look out over the bay. Caitlin stood silently beside him, her hand in his, her shoulder pressed comfortingly against his arm. High overhead, the starlike speck of a satellite moved across the sky.

Her love for him seemed to swell like an ocean wave, and she was happy to have even this brief time with him.

Suddenly Reyn dropped her hand and, cupping her shoulders, turned her toward him. Moonlight shadowed his eyes as he looked at her upturned face. Slowly he lowered his head.

Her heartbeat quickened sharply as his mouth touched hers. Her lips melted into the warmth of his, clinging as his hands tightened on her shoulders and pulled her closer.

His mouth caressed hers, the tip of his tongue lightly stroking, enticing her to a deeper response. It came quickly, and she pressed against him, letting her awakening passion take control. Her tongue darted against his and she felt him shudder.

Just when she thought she couldn't bear for him to stop, he pushed back. Then, as if powerless to resist, he lowered his head again for one last quick stinging kiss. Caitlin's lips clung to his, but she felt his internal struggle for control. She pulled away, breathing quickly, her eyes wide and blurred with desire. Until this moment, she'd never really understood what it was like to want someone, wholly, without reservation.

Reyn stared at her for a long moment, his eyes darkened by more than the night. The line between his brows cut deep. Finally he forced a smile.

"The moonlight made me do it," he said lightly, as though needing an excuse.

Caitlin's smile was a little shaky and her senses were still reeling from the shock of her intense arousal. "Oh?" she said, striving for a teasing note. If he wanted to treat this lightly, then so would she. Somehow. "It's only a half-moon. What happens when it's full?"

Reyn growled and his smile vanished. "I go animal. You're playing with fire, kid." His voice was deep with warning, then he turned abruptly. "Let's get back."

He moved away without waiting for her. After a moment, Caitlin followed. It was pretty obvious he wasn't happy about having kissed her. She supposed she could understand that. He knew she was inexperienced and she'd made it plain she was waiting for the right man, one with whom she could plan a future. He knew full well she didn't want an affair...and yet, he'd been tempted by her response to his kisses.

THEY SAT WITH THEIR BACKS resting against a sea-polished log, the fire in front of them. Strips of fog rose from the ground, thickening until they muffled the night. The ocean became a soft distorted murmur in the background.

Midnight had passed. The deer moved a few steps higher on the beach before lying down again, just beyond the flicker of firelight.

Caitlin leaned forward, lacing her fingers around her knees. She was damp, cold and sleepy on the outside. Inside she felt warm, alive and glowing. Just thinking of Reyn's kisses brought a smile.

Reyn's ill temper hadn't lasted. The tension between them had been slow to dissipate, but it had. Their first few attempts at conversation were rather stilted, but at last things felt normal again. Or almost normal. Still, she couldn't erase the memory of his lips on hers. It played over and over again in her mind. She sighed softly.

Reyn looked up. "Tired?"

"Sleepy," she murmured, not quite meeting his eyes.

"You could go up to the house."

She shook her head. "It's too much trouble."

He moved closer to her. "Then rest against me." He put an arm around her and pulled her back.

She rested her head on his shoulder, very aware of his closeness . . . of how much she loved him.

Would the caresses they'd shared under the moonlight have gone further if they'd been in the comfort of the house? If Reyn had tried to make love to her, would she have stopped him? *Could* she have stopped him? She thought of how he'd made her feel and doubted it.

She longed for him to kiss her again. She wanted to feel the length of his body press against hers without the bulk of winter clothing between them. She wanted to feel his hands on her body, caressing her breasts, cupping her hips and pulling closer to his... She drew a sharp breath at the thought.

"Something wrong?" Reyn asked.

Caitlin shook her head, her cheek rubbing against his shoulder. "I'm just tired," she murmured, suppressing a sigh of contentment as he tightened his arm around her protectively.

"Sleep for a while. I'll keep watch."

Caitlin closed her eyes, but it was to savor his closeness, not to sleep.

CHAPTER SIX

IT WAS CLOSE to four in the morning by the time the deer regained the strength to move on. Reyn put out the fire as Caitlin packed up, then they started back to the house.

"She'll be okay, won't she?" Caitlin asked, looking to where the deer had picked her way into the dark shelter of trees rimming the shore.

"Let's hope so. Maybe she'll be a little more wary the next time and manage to avoid getting chased like that." He draped an arm over her shoulders. "C'mon, kid. Let's get home."

Damp and cold, and more than a little stiff, Caitlin went with him, trudging wearily through the sand, following the bobbing beam of the flashlight.

As soon as they were in the house, she murmured a quick good-night and slipped into her room, too tired for the hot bath she'd promised herself. After shedding her damp clothes, she pulled on her pajamas and crawled into bed. It had never felt so warm and comfortable. She tucked the covers under her chin and closed her eyes.

She slept deeply for a few hours and awoke feeling refreshed and alert.

Lying on her back with one arm behind her head, she stared up at the ceiling. What would it be like facing Reyn in the revealing light of day?

Last night, cocooned in the firelit darkness by a blanket of fog, it hadn't been hard to hide from him what she felt. Today it might not be so easy, especially if he wanted to paint her. Could she sit under those perceptive eyes of his and not reveal her love? Moaning softly, she turned onto her side and curled her legs up. It wouldn't be easy. And if he should kiss her again, it would be impossible not to respond. All she felt for him would burst forth with just one touch of his lips on hers.

Every instinct warned her not to let that happen. An affair with Reyn would be disastrous for her well-being.

BY THE TIME she'd showered, dried her hair and dressed, it was midmorning. Taking a deep calming breath, she walked quietly into the living room, only to find it empty. Sighing with a mixture of relief and disappointment, she went into the kitchen.

The coffee had been made, and Rex was at the back door scratching to be let in. Reyn was obviously up, she realized as she opened the door for the dog. Where was he? She poured herself a cup of coffee and stood with her back to the counter, drinking it, and thinking again of the passion he'd stirred in her. She couldn't help but want to feel his touch again.

Reyn came down the hall from his room. Her stomach muscles clenched nervously, but she managed to return his smile. The strength of her feeling for him terrified her. *He must sense something,* she thought, with a rising sense of panic. *He must.*

"Good morning," she said, looking down at the coffee remaining in her cup, then up again. In spite of herself, her uncertainty was reflected in her eyes.

"Good morning," Reyn returned. He stooped down and gave the dog a quick pat. "Caitlin . . ."

"Mmm?" She took a sip of coffee.

"I've got to go," he said, straightening.

"Go where?" she asked, forcing her voice to sound natural.

"Victoria. There was a message on the answering machine from the art dealer who handles my work. He wants to meet with me. It looks like I'm going to have a showing of my work in Toronto, with a good possibility of it traveling to New York, then on to Washington. He's putting it together now."

Caitlin put down her cup and leaned against the counter. "That sounds great. When would it be?"

"February, from the sounds of it. And that means a lot of organization, starting immediately. Allan wants me in Victoria as soon as possible—we've got to decide which paintings we want to show and make arrangements to borrow certain ones already sold. He's very efficient, but he needs my input, the sooner the better."

Reyn was leaving. Her time on the island was ending. "Congratulations," she said evenly, managing a smile. "It sounds like a wonderful opportunity. When are you off?"

"I want to catch the twelve-thirty ferry."

She nodded and stood up. "I'll go pack my things."

Reyn shook his head quickly, stopping her with a hand on her arm. "Caitlin . . . wait. I want you to stay until I get back."

She turned to face him, frowning slightly. "Reyn, I've got to get back to Vancouver. I've already stayed here a lot longer than I should."

He pulled her into his arms and held her close, smiling down at her. "You haven't stayed nearly long enough," he said huskily. His hands dropped to her waist and with a quick movement he lifted her onto the counter. Of their own accord, her hands crept up to rest on his shoulders, and she looked at him, her eyes shy and wide with surprise.

"I know I should keep my distance," he muttered, tracing the outline of her lips with gentle fingers. "For both our sakes. You're such an innocent—and so damned irresistible."

Caitlin scarcely heard his words. At that moment, all she wanted in this world was his kiss. She saw her need echoed in the warm melting darkness of his eyes as his mouth claimed hers.

It was different from the exploring kiss they'd shared on the fog-bound beach. Reyn's mouth was hard and demanding, and with a little moan, she answered his passion.

Growling deep in his throat, he pulled her closer to the edge of the counter. Her knees parted and she melded to the thrust of his hips as she wrapped her arms around his neck. Any thought of stopping him fled. This was the man she loved, the only man she had ever wanted. Pressing impossibly closer, she kissed him with a passion that swelled from hidden depths.

Reyn pulled back abruptly. Startled, Caitlin looked at him through half-closed eyes.

"Reyn?" she whispered.

"Sorry, Caitlin" he said roughly. "Bad timing." He rubbed a thumb over her swollen bottom lip. "Oh, but how I want you," he said, his voice taut with suppressed passion.

Caitlin looked down, her lashes dark against flushed cheeks. She had never seen such blatant desire in a man's eyes before. The promise in them made her aware of just how much she yearned for him to continue.

"I must be crazy... but, stay, Caitlin," he whispered. "I want you here when I get back."

"Reyn, no. It's time for me to leave." Her protest was halfhearted and he knew it.

He ran a hand over her hair, then wove a glossy strand through his fingers. "Don't deny what you're feeling. Stay," he murmured. He smiled crookedly. "Do it for Rex—he needs someone to look after him while I'm gone. Either you stay or it's the kennel for him again. He hates it."

His eyes held hers, and she read the promises implicit in their depths. When he returned, he would take her to his bed, make impassioned love to her again and again... Her breath caught in her throat as reason struggled with emotion. "Reyn, I—"

He stopped her words with a kiss. "Stay, Caitlin," he urged, his lips warm against hers. "Wait for me."

Her love for him won out. Her gaze fluttered down to the clean-shaven jut of his jaw then back to his eyes. She sighed as she nodded. "All right. I'll stay."

"Great." He moved as though to kiss her again, but pulled away instead, his brow creased. "Caitlin, you know how much I hate to leave."

She nodded again as she slid from the countertop to stand beside him. She knew how much he wanted her. Inexperience didn't mean naïveté.

He jammed his hands in his pockets and looked at her through heavy-lidded eyes. "We've been working toward a showing like this for a long time," he said. "It's important that we get things rolling as quickly as possible. But I should be back by Friday."

He started to move away, but instead turned back to her. Unable to resist the light of passion in his eyes, she reached up and wrapped her arms around his neck, pressing her pliant body to his. With a groan of desire, he clasped her tightly, his lips and tongue caressing hers. At last, he pushed away.

"Promise me you'll stay," he said gruffly.

"Yes," she whispered, wanting him. Hugging her arms to her chest, she looked away from the blaze of desire in his eyes. "You'd better go."

He exhaled harshly. "While I still can."

She felt the fleeting touch of his hand on her hair, then heard his footsteps retreat down the hall. Without thinking she ran to the back entrance and grabbed her coat, pushing open the door.

When she could no longer see the house, she sank down against the rough bark of a cedar tree and looked out over the ocean. It wasn't long before she heard Reyn start his car. As the sound of the engine faded in the distance, she heard a low mournful howling as Rex protested his master's departure.

Feeling entirely sympathetic, she got up and went to comfort him.

IF IT HADN'T BEEN for Rex, Caitlin would have left before Friday. Time and distance had encouraged a return to sanity. Without Reyn's intoxicating presence, reason could be heard again. As she spent the days walking along the beach and the long nights in front of the fire, Caitlin had plenty of time to think.

She'd always assumed—hoped—that the man she fell in love with would love her in return. She'd taken it for granted that would mean the commitment of marriage and, eventually, a family.

Was Reyn in love with her? She honestly didn't think so. Until he'd succumbed to the moment on the moonlit beach and kissed her, he'd given no indication that he thought of her romantically at all. His kiss had sparked the desire she'd begun to feel, and her response had kindled an awareness in him. He'd reacted to her passion with a passion of his own. And there was her untouched sexuality—she sensed it made him cautious. But she sensed, too, that it held an attraction for him.

What he felt for her was surely more than sexual—but it wasn't love.

Caitlin knew she had two choices. She could let Reyn know as soon as he returned that she'd changed her mind. Or she could take him as her lover knowing she could expect little more than an affair, one that would slowly die once she left his home. She knew which option would hurt less, but she wasn't sure that was the choice she wanted to make.

Before Reyn there had been no one she'd wanted to become involved with. And she knew that even time and distance wouldn't diminish what she felt for him. She loved him. And it would be a long while—if ever—before she'd feel that way about someone else. Reyn didn't love her, and she could see no future in a relationship with him, but maybe she should take what he *could* offer her. At least she would have the memories.

She knew how he felt. She knew what she could expect from him. She wouldn't go into the relationship with expectations of a happy ending. That would make the final break less painful, wouldn't it? Deep down she knew she was fooling herself. It already hurt to know he wouldn't always be in her life.

She didn't hear from Reyn until Thursday. There was a message waiting on the answering machine when she returned from a walk with the dog. She rewound the tape and listened.

He would be coming back on Friday, later than he'd expected. He wanted to take her out for a birthday supper and she was to meet him in the lounge of the restaurant in Courtenay where she'd gone with Gabby. And she should bring an overnight bag. Friends of his were having a party and he'd promised to attend. Because of the ferry schedule, he'd made arrangements for them to spend the night.

Caitlin was frowning when she switched off the machine. She wished Reyn had left a number. Then she could have phoned him back to tell him she didn't want to go along with his plans. Meeting him for supper was one thing. Showing up afterward at a house full of his friends—strangers to her—was another.

She lit the fire, then paced while the flames caught and sent their light flickering around the room. Where had he arranged for them to stay the night? With his friends, or at a hotel? And had he made sure of separate accommodations, or did he expect her to share with him? She sat down abruptly, scowling into the fire. Earlier she wouldn't have thought it possible, but suddenly everything was even more complicated.

As she sat there, she came to realize once and for all that she must not sleep with Reyn. No matter how powerful her physical responses to him were, they shouldn't be acted upon. As she'd known in her heart all along, an affair would be wrong for her.

Friday morning she gathered up her belongings and packed. Her stay on the island was coming to an end. She had just over a week of sick leave left. It was time she returned to Vancouver and got on with her life. She would have dinner with Reyn and meet his friends afterward, if that was what he wanted. She would even spend the night if that made things easier for him. But only if they had separate rooms.

She was determined not to sleep with him. As much as she wanted him, longed to experience his love-making, she knew she had to keep that final distance between them. Life was going to be empty without him. Memories of being held in his arms, lost to his touch wouldn't help. They would make her even more aware of how little she had without his love.

REYN WAS WAITING FOR HER in the restaurant lounge, nursing a drink. As he looked up, his dark eyes narrowed intently as they swept over her.

One glance told her that he still wanted her, and her own desire surfaced in an uncontrollable rush. Her hard-won resolve came to nothing in his presence. Her eyes were wide and luminous, her face flushed as she crossed the room to where he sat.

He rose to greet her, taking her hands in his. "Caitlin," he said huskily and dropped a quick kiss on her parted lips. "You look beautiful."

"Thank you," she murmured. Pulling her hands from his, she took her seat, her lashes sweeping down, then up again as she looked at him with a shy smile. "How did it go?" she asked, her voice softly breathless.

"Very well. It took a couple of thousand phone calls—at least, it felt like it. But things are rolling now. Allan can handle the rest."

He took her hand again and raised it to his lips, pressing a kiss on her knuckles. "Miss me?"

Caitlin felt her color rise with her quickening heartbeat. "Rex did," she said, striving for even tones. "He howled for an hour after you left."

"Only because he wanted a car ride. Miss me?" he repeated, his eyes laughing as her color deepened.

"I missed your cooking," she said. "I haven't had a decent meal since you left. Can we eat soon?"

Chuckling, Reyn leaned back in his chair. "Do you want a drink first?"

"No, thank you."

He signaled the waiter. "Then let's go eat. Our table is ready."

REYN CLINKED his brandy snifter against hers. "Happy birthday."

Caitlin smiled, relaxed after an excellent meal and the pleasure of his company. "Thank you."

"I bought you a present," he continued. "But it wasn't something I could bring in here with me. I'll give it to you tomorrow."

"What is it?"

He grinned and shook his head. "Uh-uh. You can wait."

"No, I can't. Give me a hint, Reyn."

His eyes were full of laughter. "It isn't bigger than a bread box and it's either animal, vegetable or mineral."

Caitlin sighed and shook her head in mock exasperation. "That really narrows it down. I should be able to guess it sometime before the end of the century."

He took a sip of brandy, then set his glass down on the table. He reached for her hand, closing his warm fingers around hers. "Patience, Caitlin, patience."

Caitlin looked down, unable to meet his eyes, knowing he was talking about much more than the gift.

"I wish I could get out of this party," he muttered, his voice low and intimate. "I want to take you home with me." His thumb caressed the skin on the back of her hand. "Tonight. Right now."

Caitlin licked her lips nervously and risked a quick look. His meaning was very clear. He wanted to finish what they'd started.

Was she ready? Physically, she was more than ready. Emotionally, she still didn't think she could handle it—not the aftermath, the day when she'd be forced to recognize that their time together had come to an end.

"What is it, Caitlin?" he asked, watching her thoughts flicker across her face.

She raised her shoulders in a shrug and smiled. All her concerns for the future dimmed when she looked into his eyes and saw the promise of passion in their depths.

"Nothing," she said lightly. "I guess I'm just a little anxious about meeting your friends."

He gave her hand a reassuring squeeze. "Don't worry about it. They'll love you." He picked up his glass and swallowed the last of his brandy. "And speaking of the party, it's about time we left."

CAITLIN FOLLOWED REYN in her car, parking just behind his on a suburban street in Comox. The house overlooked the bay and the valley beyond. Lights twinkled in the still night and trailed across the water.

The hosts were a friendly middle-aged couple, Wes and Edie Wilhelm. Edie welcomed Reyn with a kiss on the cheek, Wes with a hearty handshake. They looked curiously at Caitlin, but greeted her with warmth.

Edie took Caitlin's overnight bag from Reyn. "This way, Caitlin. I'll show you to your room, then introduce you to everyone."

Caitlin followed the plump gray-haired woman to an upstairs room. She could hear music and laughter coming from an open staircase leading to the basement.

"Reyn's room is just down the hall," Edie volunteered as she opened the bedroom door. "He didn't say anything, but I thought I'd better put you in separate bedrooms, just in case." She flicked on the overhead light and smiled at Caitlin. "You're welcome to change things if you want."

"Oh, no, this is just fine," Caitlin said hastily. "Reyn and I are just friends."

Edie laughed. "I kind of wondered. You don't look much like his usual girlfriends. Not," she added quickly, "that there have been that many of them, but they do seem to be variations of the same theme.

"This was my daughter's room," Edie continued, gesturing with a dimpled hand. "She's in university now. We haven't made it into a spare room yet. She still comes home once a month or so."

It looked like a teenager's room. The walls were covered with posters of rock stars, and a desk overflowed with plush animals.

Edie put down the case and turned to Caitlin, a smile lighting her hazel eyes. "The bathroom is just down the hall. There are towels on the dresser. Just make yourself at home."

Caitlin smiled back at her a little shyly. "Thank you. It's very nice of you to put me up like this."

Edie waved a hand dismissively. "Any friend of Reyn's is welcome." She crossed her arms over her ample bosom and leaned against the dresser, tilting her head to one side. "I have to admit to being very curious about you, Caitlin." She grinned suddenly. "I may ask a lot of questions."

Caitlin responded to her warmth. "Ask away," she said with a laugh.

"For starters, how long have you known Reyn?"

"Not long. Actually, I'm a friend of Gabrielle's. I was staying in the cabin near Reyn's, but it turned out to be rather uncomfortable, so he asked me to stay with him, instead.''

Edie nodded. ''So you really *are* just friends.'' She saw the look on Caitlin's face and hurried to explain. ''I only ask because Stevie Hayes is coming tonight. She and Reyn used to have a thing going. As far as I know, it's been over for a while. Still, I thought things might get a little awkward.''

''Don't worry about it,'' Caitlin said lightly, masking her sudden disappointment. She didn't want Stevie here tonight. ''I've already met her.''

''That's good. I'd hate to think there was any conflict. So, are you ready to meet the others?''

Caitlin nodded, hoping her reluctance didn't show. She would much rather just stay where she was.

Edie sensed her hesitation. ''Don't worry. They're all nice people. A real mixture, everything from artists to accountants.'' She straightened up and inclined her head toward the doorway. ''Let's go.''

Caitlin smoothed her skirt with damp palms and followed her hostess.

TIRED OF MAKING CONVERSATION, Caitlin found a quiet corner and nursed a drink, watching the others. Lights had been dimmed in the large family room, and the stereo turned up. Several couples were dancing to old rock songs.

Reyn had been at her side for most of the evening. He'd kept a possessive hand on her arm as he introduced her to everyone and made no mention of the fact she was Gabby's friend. His attention had made her feel warm and wanted. And then Stevie had arrived.

He hadn't abandoned Caitlin straight away. But when Stevie approached him, he'd turned to her immediately, frowning when he saw the tight look on her face. Then he'd taken her off to a quiet corner, leaving Caitlin talking to a young art teacher.

A slow burn of jealousy started deep inside. Stevie was still very much a part of Reyn's life, both personally and professionally. It bothered Caitlin to see them together and she'd had a hard time keeping her mind on what the art teacher was saying.

Eventually she'd drifted off to refill her glass with a drink she didn't really want. She watched as Reyn sat on the arm of Stevie's chair, leaning forward to catch what she was saying. The conversation seemed intense and personal.

Caitlin knew they were no longer lovers. That now, at least as far as Reyn was concerned, they were merely friends with business ties. And friendship did seem to be what Reyn was offering Stevie, she told herself firmly, fighting off the gnawing jealousy. There were no smoldering looks between them, no caresses disguised as casual touches.

Just as Caitlin had decided to slip off to her room, Edie approached. Her eyes darted from Reyn and Stevie to Caitlin's face. "If you're worrying about Stevie, don't. It's been over between them for quite some time. I think it's their interest in art that keeps them friends as much as anything, as well as the fact that Stevie does Reyn's framing for him."

Caitlin managed a brief smile. It was disconcerting to watch the man she loved with his former lover, no matter what the reason. It was hard to pretend it didn't bother her, that Reyn was just a friend. And Edie had sensed that.

"Stevie is going through a bit of a bad time just now. I think she needs Reyn's advice." Edie hesitated and then continued, "I'm not sure exactly what it's all about, but I do know she's met someone else, and that he seems to care a lot for her. Maybe she just needs to know it's really over between her and Reyn before she can move on to another relationship."

Caitlin took a sip of her drink. It was all a little much for her, the way Stevie could ask for advice from her former lover before taking on a new one.

Edie gave her hand a reassuring pat. "Don't worry about it," she said again. "Talk to me, instead." She chuckled. "Reyn probably warned you—I love to know everything about everybody. So tell me about yourself. For starters, what do you do?"

Caitlin responded to Edie's warmth. The older woman seemed genuinely interested in hearing about Caitlin's class, expressing sympathy over the children's problems. Distracted, Caitlin didn't notice Reyn until he was at her side.

He grinned at Edie, his dark eyes teasing. "If you're finished with the third degree, Edie, can I dance with Caitlin?"

"I just asked a few harmless questions," Edie said, raising her eyebrows haughtily. "Nothing that would embarrass you."

"Nothing ever embarrasses me." He held out a hand to Caitlin. "Dance with me?"

He led her to where several couples were dancing to a slow swaying beat and took her in his arms. Moving stiffly, Caitlin stared at the swirl of pattern on his sweater.

"Hey, relax," Reyn said. He hooked a finger under her chin and raised her face until she was looking at him. He smiled warmly. "Enjoying yourself?"

She lowered her eyes and nodded, more polite than sincere. Whatever enjoyment she'd felt had fled with Stevie's arrival.

Reyn rubbed a thumb over her bottom lip, smiling at the color rising in her cheeks. When she pulled away from his hand, resting her head on his chest to hide her revealing face, he played with a soft glossy strand of her hair.

Giving herself up to the moment, Caitlin relaxed, feeling the steady thud of his heart against her cheek. Her body followed the beat of the music, moving against his. For a few brief moments, she was aware of nothing else. She was in his arms, where she longed to be.

But not here. Reality trickled in and made itself heard. Not dancing in a room full of people. Not with his former lover nearby.

Stevie's presence made the future all too clear. In a few months, it could just as easily be Caitlin watching from the side as Reyn danced with the new woman in his life. She couldn't do that to herself. She put a hand on his chest and pushed herself back a little.

"What's the matter?" Reyn murmured.

She gave him an apologetic smile. "I'm tired," she said. "I think I'll go to bed."

Reyn raised his eyebrows. "So soon? It won't be very quiet, Caitlin. This is going to go on for a while yet."

"It's okay. I . . . I've got a bit of a headache. Lying down will help." She needed to be alone, away from Reyn so she could think—rethink—things over.

"Are you sure?"

She nodded, slipping out of his arms.

"Wait. I'll get a couple of aspirin from Edie."

"It's okay. I have some in my purse. Would you say good-night to her for me, please?"

"Later. I'll go up with you." He took her arm and guided her across the floor to the stairs.

As they left the room, Caitlin caught a glimpse of Stevie standing in a darkened corner, watching them.

Reyn put his hands on her shoulders when they reached her door, and looked closely at her. Her face was pale, her eyes troubled. "Will you be all right?"

"I just need some sleep," she murmured, staring at his chest. "Good night."

"Caitlin..." He hesitated, then dropped a light kiss on her cheek. "Sleep well," he said. "I'll see you in the morning."

Caitlin slipped into the room and shut the door behind her, aware that Reyn still hadn't left to rejoin the party. She leaned against the door until she heard his footsteps retreat down the hall. Sighing, she rubbed a hand across her brow and crossed the room to sit on the bed.

Her head really did ache. And her shoulders were stiff with tension. She didn't have the experience or sophistication to handle a situation like this. It bothered her to see Stevie and Reyn together. Not just out of jealousy, not really. She honestly didn't think that there was anything going on between them. Not anymore.

What Stevie's presence did was show Caitlin all too clearly what the progression of her own relationship with Reyn would be.

She couldn't handle it. She couldn't live for the moment the way her mother did, knowing that when one relationship was over, another was just around the corner. Caitlin's entire childhood had been one of impermanence, lived in the tail wind of her mother's whims; new towns, new schools, different and yet all too similar men to call Uncle.

There was a strong physical resemblance between Caitlin and her mother, and she'd grown up hearing people marvel at how much alike they were. Caitlin knew just how wrong that was, yet a tiny part of her feared that if she wasn't careful, her life might parallel her mother's.

She might love Reyn more than her mother had loved any man, but she knew that her involvement with him would be temporary. One day, sooner or later, it would be over. And then what would happen? Would she find herself becoming more and more like her mother, drifting from man to man in a futile attempt to recapture what she'd had with Reyn?

Caitlin shuddered at the thought. No, she'd do best to keep to her resolve. If Reyn couldn't give her all she needed, then she would take nothing. She wouldn't live the kind of life her mother had—she couldn't do that to herself.

Caitlin did little more than doze through the night, and it was early when she gave up the fight and got out of bed. She washed quietly and dressed in jeans and a sweatshirt before going tentatively into the kitchen.

She'd thought she could help out by cleaning up some of the party's debris, but there was nothing out of place in the gleaming kitchen. A quick look in the family room showed that it, too, had been cleaned.

Back in the kitchen, Caitlin turned on the coffee maker and sat quietly at the table looking out the window and waiting for the coffee to brew.

"Good morning." Edie stood smiling in the doorway, her short curly hair still damp from her shower. She wore a loose gray sweat suit and floppy red slippers on her feet.

"Good morning." Caitlin returned her smile easily. "It's a beautiful day."

"Isn't it?" Edie took two mugs from the cupboard and filled them with coffee. "I'm thankful for every day the sun shines at this time of the year. Cream and sugar?"

"Just cream, please." Caitlin turned back to look out the window. "This is a perfect view."

Edie nodded as she placed a mug of steaming coffee in front of Caitlin. Then she sat down opposite and stirred a spoonful of sugar into her coffee. "That was quite a party last night. I was beginning to think no one would ever leave. Not that I minded," she added. "I enjoy having people over."

"It was nice," Caitlin agreed. She added a bit more cream to her coffee and stirred it in. "I thought I would help clean up this morning, but it was all done."

"Wes tidied up while he was waiting for Reyn to come back from taking Stevie home. She'd had a bit too much to drink and we didn't want her driving," Edie explained. She caught the expression that flitted across Caitlin's face.

"Caitlin, I don't know you very well, but Reyn's been a friend—a good friend—for years. He's not in love with Stevie. I think at first he hoped he would be, but it didn't work out. You don't have anything to worry about."

"We really are just friends," Caitlin said, trying to keep her voice light. Was she so transparent?

"So you say, but after last night, I get the feeling Reyn doesn't think so." Edie grinned. "In fact, I'm sure he doesn't."

Caitlin's smile was a little apologetic. "But I do," she said quietly. And she meant it. She took another swallow of her coffee, then glanced at the clock on the wall. "I should just be able to make the next ferry."

Edie's eyebrows lifted in surprise. "Aren't you going to wait for Reyn?"

Caitlin shook her head as she stood up. "I've got my own car."

"Well, at least wait until you've had breakfast. Reyn should be up by then."

"I'm really not hungry yet. Thanks, anyway, Edie." She took her cup to the sink and rinsed it. Turning around, she smiled at the older woman. "And thanks for your hospitality. I enjoyed meeting your friends." She looked at the clock again and started for the doorway. "I'll go get my things." She left the room, conscious of Edie watching her. Edie, Caitlin knew, thought she should stay. But she wanted some privacy the next time she faced Reyn. She needed to tell him that their relationship had gone as far as she wanted it to—and that wasn't going to be easy.

After watching him with Stevie last night, the phrase "Off with the old and on with the new" kept running through her mind. It made her a little bit angry. That was her mother's life-style. She herself didn't play that game. For her own self-preservation, she couldn't, no matter how tempted she might be.

CHAPTER SEVEN

CAITLIN STOPPED PACING and sat down as soon as she heard Reyn's car pull into the driveway. She picked up a book and flipped through it in an effort to look occupied. The words on the pages were meaningless. All her senses were tuned to Reyn's entrance.

"Caitlin?" Reyn came through the door holding a hamperlike carrying case. Rex trotted beside him, snuffling the basket.

"There you are. I thought you'd wait for me this morning."

Caitlin closed the book and laid it on the table. "I was up early. I thought I'd get back and rescue Rex. Poor thing—he hates being tied up." Her voice might have sounded calm and relaxed, but her heart was beating anxiously. How long could she hide her feelings from him?

Reyn, fortunately, seemed to notice nothing of her inner struggle.

He set the basket down in front of her. "Here's your birthday present," he said, smiling warmly. "Just as promised."

Caitlin looked at the basket. "What is it?"

"Open it and find out." Reyn sat down in the chair opposite her, a restraining hand on Rex's collar.

Caitlin pulled the basket closer and undid the clasp. "It's alive, isn't it," she said, looking at Reyn suspiciously.

He grinned at her. "I certainly hope so."

"Is it all coiled up and ready to spring?"

He chuckled. "It's entirely possible. Open it and find out."

Gingerly she lifted the lid. Inside, curled on a bit of old blanket, was a tiny Siamese kitten. As she exclaimed in delight, it opened its blue eyes and blinked. Caitlin scooped it from the basket and cuddled it under her chin.

"Oh, Reyn! It's beautiful. Thank you."

Reyn sat back in his chair, a pleased look on his face. "Her name is Lily. She's two months old and basically trained. I've got all the supplies you'll need in the car."

"I've thought about getting a kitten a few times, but never got around to it. I'm going to enjoy her. Thank you, Reyn," she said again, and gave him a happy smile.

"It was the eyes that did it. The blue is a shade deeper, but the shape and expression are just the same as yours."

"From a dog to a cat," Caitlin murmured, stroking the small wheat-colored body with gentle fingers. "Is that an improvement?"

"We'll see how the painting turns out."

Startled, Caitlin looked at him. She had been waiting for him to return so she could tell him she was leaving. Her bags were packed and waiting by her bedroom door. "Reyn, I—I wasn't planning on staying any longer."

Reyn was watching her through half-closed eyes, his mouth set. "I had a feeling you were going to say that." His voice was tinged with impatience. "Why do you have to leave?"

Caitlin unhooked tiny claws from her sweatshirt and placed the kitten on her lap. "I start back to school in just over a week. I've got to prepare for it."

"I'm sure you've got that well in hand." He tugged at Rex's collar as the dog leaned closer to the kitten, ears pointed sharply forward. "Give me another reason, Caitlin."

She looked down at the kitten playing on her lap and caught her bottom lip between her teeth. She could prevaricate all day, but she had a feeling Reyn knew exactly why she wanted to leave.

She let the kitten drag a raspy tongue over her forefinger as she tried to come up with the right words. "It's just I'm not comfortable with..." Her voice trailed off and she sighed softly, wishing it wasn't so hard to speak the simple truth.

"You don't want me to make love to you, is that it?" The words were blunt, but indulgence had replaced the impatience in his voice.

Caitlin fought down a surge of embarrassment. If two people were on the verge of becoming intimate, they should be able to talk about it. "No, I don't," she said quietly, her cheeks awash with color.

"I could change your mind."

"I know," she whispered. It would take such a small touch to melt her resolve. "Please don't."

Reyn sighed in resignation and nodded slowly. "You have my word, Caitlin. As long as you don't want to make love, we won't, and much as I want to, it's probably just as well. You're so young, so vulnerable. You have something special to offer and you should keep waiting for that right man to come along, complete with rose-covered cottage and white picket fence."

Caitlin heard the cynicism underlining his words and wished it all could be different. He'd never know it, but *he* was the right man for her. If only she could be the woman for him.

He was silent for a moment, then went on, "But I still want to paint you."

Caitlin looked at him with luminous eyes. "Reyn, don't you think it would be best if I just left?"

He grinned crookedly. "No."

She shook her head and sighed. "Reyn..."

"Indulge me," he urged. "I like having you here and I'm serious about doing another painting. C'mon, kid. Stay till the end of the week."

"I—"

"Say yes, Caitlin."

It was so easy to give in, to postpone the inevitable break as long as possible. "Okay," she agreed, wondering if she was making the right decision. "I'll stay." Was she only letting herself in for more heartbreak?

"Great. Now, let's introduce Rex to Lily before he hurts himself."

Relaxing his grip on the collar, Reyn let the dog move toward the kitten on Caitlin's lap. Eyes sharp with curiosity, Rex inched closer. Hissing, the kitten arched its back and took a swipe at the approaching nose with a tiny chocolate-colored paw. Startled, Rex backed off quickly.

Reyn rubbed the dog's ruff. "It's okay, boy," he said and added with a forlorn expression, "I know exactly how you feel."

Caitlin looked from the dog to Reyn and a giggle escaped her lips. Reyn smiled ruefully at her.

"Friends again?" he asked, holding out his hand.

Caitlin slipped her hand into his, enjoying the warmth of his clasp. "Friends again," she said, but the words nearly stuck in her throat. It was no longer enough.

CAITLIN KNEW that Reyn would keep his word. He wouldn't make love to her unless it was what she wanted. But she also knew she was playing with fire. Because no matter how hard she fought it, she wanted him. It was an ever-present gnawing ache.

She watched him as he stepped back from the canvas in front of him. He took off his glasses and rubbed the stem across his bottom lip, frowning in concentration. Did he have any idea just how much she wanted him to make love to her, how tentative her resolve that he wouldn't? She had a feeling he probably did. Her inexperience kept him at bay. He might be attracted by it, but he would hold off if that was what she wanted.

"It's not right," he said suddenly, shaking his head as he looked at the painting. "Something's missing." He looked back to where she sat holding the kitten on her lap. "The faces side by side worked with Rex, but we need something different with the cat. Cats are sinuous. Sensual. I should be using that. Maybe curled up by the fire. Firelight reflecting on your— Hang on a sec." He turned and walked quickly from the room, the line between his eyes cutting deep.

Smiling, Caitlin put the kitten down and went to look out the window. Rain streaked steadily down the glass and the trees bowed to a persistent northerly wind. She enjoyed seeing Reyn caught in the spell of creativity. She loved knowing that his eyes were on her and her alone, intimate eyes, safely distanced by the canvas between them.

Reyn came back into the room. "Here. Go put this on."

It was a black satin robe. Caitlin took it, her eyebrows raised, and looked at him. "Black satin? Really, Reyn," she murmured.

He grinned. "Black satin and firelight..." He snapped his fingers. "A crystal glass of red wine." He strode toward the kitchen, adding, "Try it on over your clothes."

Caitlin shook out the folds in the robe and slipped it on. It was big on her, and she tied the sash tightly to keep it from sliding down over her shoulders. As she freed her hair from the collar, she caught a faint scent of musky perfume and grimaced. Which one of his lovers had the robe belonged to?

Reyn came back carrying a glass of wine. He stopped and looked at her critically.

Caitlin held out her arms and twirled around. "It's too big."

"A bit," Reyn agreed, setting the wineglass down on the coffee table. "And we could do without the sweatshirt underneath. But it looks good." He tilted his head to one side and looked her over, grinning suddenly when he saw the tips of her fuzzy sky-blue socks peaking out from under the sleek material. "The socks will definitely have to go."

Caitlin raised the hem of the robe and wriggled her toes. "My feet will freeze."

"I'll toss another log on the fire. Now, let me set things up."

REYN STOPPED after blocking the picture onto his canvas. "I'll start the painting tonight," he told Caitlin as he stretched. "I want the light from the fire fading to darkness—a shading of background. Now, what do you say to a nice long walk?"

"In the rain?"

Reyn nodded decisively. "In the rain. There's nothing like a walk along the beach on a stormy day."

Caitlin cuddled the kitten under her chin, tempted to stay where she was. "I'm warm and dry and comfortable...but okay, I'll come." It would feel good to stretch, especially if Reyn planned on painting later, and she wanted to grab every opportunity to be with him, gathering memories to carry her through the lonely times to come.

She put the purring kitten into the carrying case. "I'll get my raincoat."

They followed the road down to the bay, avoiding the rain-slick path. Wind swept through the trees, then hit the sea, whipping gray water into white-capped waves. They walked briskly to keep warm, hands jammed into pockets and faces bowed against the wind. Rex stayed close, hating the rain but unwilling to forgo a walk with his master.

Caitlin waited quietly, the dog pressed against her leg, as Reyn stopped to look out over the ocean. He stood tall, his chin thrust forward, eyes half-closed against the rain, a man inspired by the elements and the natural world around him. Her love welled in a warm aching rush. She would miss him so much.

He turned to look at her, grinning suddenly. "You're wet."

"Wet is an understatement," she said. "I'm bordering on waterlogged." Rain trickled from her hair down her face. Her eyelashes were spiked with moisture.

He ran a finger along the bridge of her nose, then lightly touched her mouth. For a moment it seemed as though he would kiss her, but he spoke instead.

"We should get back."

She nodded and gave the dog a pat, hoping she had kept her disappointment from showing. "A hot bath would feel pretty good right about now."

"And some cocoa," Reyn added as they began the return trek. "I think I'll make some sandwiches with the leftover salmon from last night."

"Mmm—sounds good. It's nice to be around someone who enjoys preparing food."

"I wouldn't know. Although you do pour milk on cereal with a fine little flair."

Caitlin gave him a poke with her elbow and made a face. "Don't be nasty. I'll make supper tomorrow." She grinned at him. "If you have any packages of macaroni-and-cheese, that is. Or frozen dinners or—"

"Never mind," he said, shaking his head. "I'll cook."

"You do it so well, Reyn," she said demurely.

He tweaked a wet strand of her hair, laughter lurking in his eyes. "Flattery will get you off the hook this time. But one of these days, *you* can wear the apron and wield the spatula."

"Frozen pizza? If I promise not to burn it?"

"Maybe I'll give you lessons," he murmured. "C'mon, kid. Let's get back. You look like a drowned rat and I'm beginning to feel like one." He took her hand in a warm clasp and they hurried home through winter's early dusk.

CAITLIN SAT CROSS-LEGGED by the fire, eating a salmon sandwich. She shared a bit of the fish with Lily, laughing as the kitten crawled over her lap, mewing anxiously for more. Looking up, she saw Rex sitting across from her, hopeful eyes following her hand as she raised the sandwich for another bite. Unable to resist, she broke off a piece and tossed it to him. He caught it deftly and swallowed, then resumed his hopeful watch.

Reyn came from the kitchen carrying steaming mugs of cocoa. He'd showered and changed into gray sweats imprinted with the University of Victoria logo. His dark hair was beginning to dry, curling over his forehead. She longed to touch it, to smooth it back from his temples.

Caitlin watched him through eyes soft with love. Smiling her thanks, she took the mug he offered her. She set it down on the hearth and gave the pleading kitten another morsel of salmon.

"I made people food, not pet food," Reyn grumbled mildly. He took a sandwich from the plate on the coffee table and bit into it.

Caitlin tossed another morsel to Rex. "I can't resist those pleading eyes," she admitted. She ate the last of her sandwich and picked up the mug of cocoa with its froth of melting marshmallow on top. "Forget it, guys," she said as the dog and kitten watched hopefully. "This one's all mine." She took a sip and sighed contentedly. "Perfect."

"It is, isn't it?" Reyn said quietly. "You know..." He stopped and shook his head. Caitlin raised her eyebrows in query, then watched as, with a last bite of sandwich, he stood up impatiently.

"Let's get started. I'll get things ready in here while you go put on the robe." He picked up the plates to take into the kitchen.

Caitlin got up slowly, rubbing the kitten's taut little belly. She put it down next to the litter box then went to her room.

"Remember—no socks!" Reyn called from the kitchen.

And no sweatshirt, she thought as she picked up the robe from her bed. She stripped down to her underwear and slipped into it. The material felt cool and deliciously smooth against her skin, and she shivered slightly as she tied the sash tightly around her waist.

Logs burned above a bed of glowing embers. Firelight caught the brass of the wood chest near the hearth and sparked in the crystal goblet of ruby wine. It shone in the auburn depths of Caitlin's hair and in the folds of the satin robe draped around her.

If it had been anybody but Reyn, Caitlin would have felt the whole thing was a setup, a scene meant to lead to seduction. But one look at the line cutting deeply between his brows told her his concentration was focused entirely on his painting. There was nothing personal in the dark eyes that looked up from the canvas and then down again to follow the stroke of his brush. It took a while, and more than one sip of wine, but Caitlin was finally able to relax.

She stroked the sleeping kitten tucked against her stomach and smiled to herself. *I feel like a houri in someone's dream,* she thought wryly and resisted the urge to pull up the collar of the robe. She picked up the pocket book lying beside her and began to read.

Her mind refused to absorb the printed words. Reyn might have distanced himself, but she wasn't able to. Tonight she felt secure, warmed by the strength of her love for him. But there was so little time left. In just two days, she would return to her life in Vancouver. It had never seemed so bleak. This too-short time with Reyn had shown her just how alone she really was. And she would be alone again, soon, for a long, long time. The thought filled her with a feeling of quiet desperation.

She would leave with the knowledge that she had made a good friend, one she would see again. She wanted so much more. Sighing, she shifted slightly.

"Tired?" Reyn asked, looking at her over the rim of his glasses.

Caitlin shook her head quickly. "I'm fine."

"It won't be too much longer. I've got most of what I need. It's the colors I want now, the reflections..." His voice trailed off as his frown of concentration returned. He rubbed the end of the brush over his bottom lip for a moment then carefully dabbed at the canvas, his attention once again on his art.

Caitlin smiled, feeling her love for him behind the gnawing ache of sadness. It seemed impossible that something that felt so right had no future, no permanent place in her life.

The kitten distracted her as it awakened and stood up to stretch, its tail and all four legs stiffening with the effort. After a quick fumbling attempt at washing, it pounced on the end of Caitlin's sash. Rex watched, ears sharp, from his position near Reyn, who glanced over to share her smile. . . .

For a moment, everything was as it should be.

CAITLIN WATCHED the dwindling flames through half-closed eyes, caught in drowsy fantasy as she relived the memory of the kisses she'd shared with Reyn. It was so easy to let her mind take her to where those kisses could have led.

Reyn was the man she loved, the only man she had ever wanted as a lover. It was so easy to imagine being held in his arms.

"Sleepy?"

Startled, Caitlin looked up to see Reyn standing in front of her, a cedar log in his hands. He pulled back the screen and fed the fire, then sat on the stone hearth, arms resting across his knees.

"No, not really," Caitlin answered slowly, watching her fingers trace the edge of the kitten's chocolate mask. "Just thinking." Dreaming, she corrected herself. Impossible dreams. She smiled faintly.

Traces of those dreams showed in her eyes.

"Caitlin . . ." Reyn's voice trailed off. He reached out, hesitated for a moment, then lightly touched her cheek.

Her breath caught. She knew she should pull away from his touch, but instead she turned her head and rested her cheek in the palm of his hand, tense with the strength of feelings she could no longer suppress. Unbidden, her lips formed a kiss and pressed it against his hand.

"Caitlin." His voice was gruff with warning.

She didn't want him to talk, she didn't want him to ask, only to succumb to the feeling of the moment. Her desire for him had grown beyond the point where rational thought could stop her. She wanted him. Now. She couldn't hold back any longer.

She looked up and met the melting darkness of his eyes. Without question, he wanted her.

He saw her silent plea and answered it without hesitation. He slid off the hearth and knelt beside her, both hands cupping her face. Slowly he leaned forward and kissed her.

With a soft sigh, Caitlin melded her lips to his, giving herself to the love she felt, tremulously unveiling her need for him. Holding nothing back, she deepened the kiss, feeling Reyn's instant response as he took control. With a little moan, she relinquished herself to the spate of desire.

Suddenly Reyn drew away. He pushed the hair back from her forehead and, unable to resist, dropped a quick kiss on her half-parted lips, feeling their instant clinging response. "I can't fight it, Caitlin," he said, his voice husky with passion. "I need to make love to you." His lips burned against the pulse in her throat.

Eyes closed, Caitlin whispered with shy determination, "I need you, too, Reyn." Whatever might lie in the future, this was what she wanted tonight.

Reyn let out a long breath and pulled her to him, cradling her head against his shoulder, rubbing his chin across her shiny cap of hair. "I want you to know that—" He was stopped by a sharp plaintive howl from the kitten as it began to climb awkwardly along his thigh.

Caitlin raised her head. In spite of the tension she was feeling, she couldn't help laughing at the sight of the kitten clinging to Reyn's leg. It looked straight up at Reyn and bared its tiny fangs in another howl.

Carefully Reyn released the claws from his sweatpants. "It's bedtime for you, Lily-puss." As he stood up with the kitten, he held out a hand to Caitlin, his eyes questioning.

Knowing she could still back out if she wanted gave Caitlin the strength she needed. She slipped her hand into his and allowed him to help her to her feet. He put an arm around her shoulders and pulled her close, giving her a swift hard kiss. Then, moving quickly, he put the kitten in the carrying case before going to turn out the lights.

Caitlin stood with her arms against her chest, watching him, wondering at herself. All the arguments she'd used to convince herself she shouldn't make love to Reyn had, in one overwhelming rush of passion, come to nothing. All she knew was how much she wanted him. She might feel trepidation, but she had no doubts. Tonight, Reyn would be her lover.

REYN LOWERED HER GENTLY onto his bed. The room was dark except for the soft flickering glow of the fireplace. Caitlin's eyes were wide and luminous as she reached up and touched Reyn's face.

He kissed her temples, her brow, then brushed his lips over hers. "I want you, Caitlin," he said softly, his eyes warm and caring. "More than anything. But I want you to be sure."

Caitlin's lashes swept down and then up again. Her body felt lush and languid, yet at the same time vibrantly aware of the man beside her. "I am," she whispered. Love for him surged through her and she said on a rush of emotion, "Oh, Reyn...I'm very, very sure."

Reyn exhaled sharply. Stretching out fully, he pulled her into his arms and held her close.

Caitlin buried her face in his shoulder, her soft curves molding intimately with the hardness of his body. When his lips found hers in a demanding kiss, she felt part of herself flow into him. She was lost...and nothing had ever felt so good.

CAITLIN LAY in Reyn's arms feeling his quiet rhythmic breathing as he slept. She stared into the darkness. There was only one thing that kept the night from being perfect. Reyn didn't return her love. Surely if he'd been feeling anything akin to what she felt, he would have said something.

She sighed and shifted slightly, feeling his arms tighten as he settled his chin on the top of her head. He'd been wonderfully gentle, restraining his own passion while he guided hers. She'd known he would be a superb lover, but still, the intensity of the feelings he'd released in her came as a surprise. And she hadn't realized that *she* could be so spontaneously passionate and willing.

But now... What happened now?

Moving slowly, Caitlin pulled away from Reyn's clasp and rolled to the edge of the bed. Pushing back the covers, she swung her legs to the floor. The room was cold. Ashen embers were all that were left of the fire. Shivering, she picked up the satin robe where it lay on the floor and slipped it on.

She went to stand by the window. Rain misted against the glass and she could see little of what lay beyond. Still, she stood there, arms hugging her chest. Tears welled in her eyes and threatened to fall. Part of her still tried to reason that she should have kept that final distance between her and Reyn. But her more primitive core was fiercely glad tonight had happened. If not for Reyn, she might have gone a lifetime without experiencing how it could be between a man and a woman. It hadn't been a mistake to let him love her.

But now what? The persistent question remained unanswered.

Caitlin brushed her cheek on the shoulder of the robe, drying a tear. She no longer caught another woman's scent on the robe. Her own had permeated the satin. How long would it be before someone else wore it?

That was the problem. She was in Reyn's life temporarily when her love for him demanded permanence.

She dashed an impatient hand across her eyes, drying them. None of this was new to her. She'd gone over it all before. Reyn hadn't led her on with empty promises. They had gone this far because it was what *she* wanted. Caitlin turned away from the window and walked back to the bed. She had what was left of the night. She would take it, gathering memories to act as a buffer for the pain that lay ahead.

Dropping the robe on the floor, she slid back into bed and pressed against Reyn's side, welcoming the heat of his body against her chilled skin. She breathed his musky male scent deeply and burrowed closer, caressing him lightly. As she felt him stir, her touches became more sure, bolder.

She felt him awaken and kissed the raspy jut of his jaw, then his lips, thrilling at his instant heady response. His hand found her breast and he rubbed his palm over the thrusting nipple. Gasping against his lips, she pushed closer, wanting him all over again.

IT WAS CLOSE TO DAWN when Caitlin slipped out of bed again. She spent a moment looking down at Reyn's sleeping face. With a sad, somewhat tired smile, she touched his cheek before turning away. Sometime during the long sleepless night she'd reached a decision. She would leave before Reyn awoke.

She dressed, packed quickly and took her suitcases into the living room, setting them beside the patio doors. Rex greeted her with a thump of his tail against the floor, then he got up slowly, stretched and yawned hugely. Caitlin gave him an absentminded pat as she checked on the kitten, then closed the top of its carrying case and carried it to the door.

Biting her bottom lip in a futile attempt to hold back tears of despair, she glanced around the room one last time. The crystal glass, still half-full of wine, sat on the hearth. Dull gray ashes, without a spark of light, lay in the fireplace. Reyn's painting sat uncovered on the easel. She took a step toward it and looked.

The sensuality of the painting didn't surprise her, not after a night in Reyn's arms. He'd captured what she'd been feeling as she lay in front of the fire, dreaming of, longing for, his touch. Would he finish it once she'd gone? She hoped so, hoped he would continue to see her as beautiful and desirable.

A note, she thought suddenly. She should leave a note. She found a pen and paper near the phone and stood indecisively. What could she say?

Finally she scribbled a brief message and signed her name. It said nothing but goodbye and thanks. It would have to do.

"I've got to go, Rex," she murmured to the dog, kneeling beside him. She rubbed his ears fondly and blinked tears from her eyes. As hard as it was to leave, it was easier this way than it would be with Reyn standing there saying goodbye while she struggled not to let him see her heart breaking. It left her, just barely, with a feeling of control.

Drawing a deep breath, she fished the car keys from her jacket pocket and turned resolutely toward the door.

Rex followed her out and she gave him one last hug before climbing into her car. A quick glance at her wristwatch told her there wasn't much time before the ferry left. Holding her breath, she started the engine, hoping the sound wouldn't wake Reyn.

She switched on the wipers and eased the car into gear. She glanced into the rearview mirror as the car began to move down the driveway. Rex sat where she had left him. He pointed his muzzle to the pewter-dull sky and began a long mournful howl. Biting her lip hard, Caitlin stepped on the gas and drove away.

CHAPTER EIGHT

IT WAS A LONG and dismal trip back to Vancouver. The ferry churned through dull gray waters that seemed a continuation of dull gray skies. As the boat pulled into Horseshoe Bay, rain began to seep from the clouds in misty strands.

Clutching the steering wheel of her car tightly, Caitlin drove like an automaton through the gloom, her neck and shoulders tight with tension. When she finally pulled into the parking space behind her apartment building, she closed her eyes and let out a deep breath, resting her forehead on the steering wheel. A sudden mewing from the basket next to her penetrated the fog of pain. She lifted the lid and stroked the kitten inside.

"We're home, Lily-puss," she murmured, then glanced at the old rain-streaked brick wall and sighed. For the first time, she didn't have a sense of coming home.

Inside was no better. She saw her apartment through new eyes. Never had it seemed so tiny, the walls so close. Through the windows came the constant buzz of city noise. Cars and trucks moved up the street in a steady stream. People darted in and out of specialty shops, and neon lights glowed brightly in the rain-dark day.

Gone was the warm feeling she'd always felt before. Dejected, she huddled on the couch, holding the kitten close, glad of its warmth and comforting purr. Tears welled, then fell from her eyes. A sense of loss washed over her and a quavering sob spilled from her throat. Her heart had found another home.

GABRIELLE STOOD in the doorway, her brown eyes thoughtful as she looked at Caitlin. "So. You're back."

"I'm back," Caitlin agreed, standing aside to let her friend enter. It was hard to act in a normal fashion. She hoped her smile didn't seem as forced as it felt. Shutting the door, she followed Gabrielle into the living room.

"How's Reyn?" Gabby asked as she flopped onto the couch.

Caitlin shrugged nonchalantly. "Okay, I suppose." She sat down, none of her pain showing. It was a struggle but she was in control again. "How are things at the school?"

"As usual, just before Christmas break. The kids are all hyped up from TV commercials, convinced Santa is going to bring them everything they want. Even those from other religions are caught up in it." She sighed a little sadly. "There'll be a lot of disappointed kids Christmas morning. I really wish Christmas would get back to the basics. Anyway, I—" She stopped in surprise as Lily strutted out of the bedroom, tiny tail held high.

"Oh, is she ever cute!" she exclaimed. "Where did you get her?"

"From Reyn." Caitlin kept her voice even. "For my birthday. Her name is Lily."

"Here kitty, kitty, kitty," Gabrielle crooned, scooping up the kitten as it approached. She cuddled it close, grinning. "That was thoughtful of him," she said, looking intently at Caitlin. "So, how is it between you two?"

Caitlin shrugged again. "Okay. He did another painting just before I left." *Before I sneaked off, afraid to face him as my lover in the light of the day.*

"And?" Gabby prompted, as though she suspected their relationship might have gone further.

"And nothing," Caitlin said, forcing herself to keep her mind on Gabby. "I got a break from the city while he painted me. That's it."

Gabby put the kitten on her knee. "I'm glad. I was hoping you had enough sense not to fall victim to his considerable charm. I'd hate to see you get hurt."

"Me, too," Caitlin said, but it was an effort. Her voice almost broke. She cleared her throat hastily and managed a smile. "I'm just not his type, I guess. I'm small and dark. I don't have an ounce of artistic talent, and I'm not involved in any conservation groups or any of the other things important to him."

Something in her manner caused Gabby to look at her closely. "Caitlin, are you sure he didn't try anything?"

"I'm sure." The last thing she wanted was for Gabby to suspect how far things had really gone. She wouldn't let it rest, Caitlin knew, and would undoubtedly light into Reyn. "I had a nice visit, and we enjoyed each other's company for a time. That's as far as it goes."

Gabby nodded, believing her. "Y'know, in a way it's too bad. You're so much more . . . *real* than some of those women he sees. It might have been nice if . . . Well, never mind."

As Gabby continued to talk about Reyn, Caitlin fought hard to keep her pain from showing. A lifetime of practice came to her aid and she managed to keep her friend from suspecting how badly she hurt, how every mention of Reyn's name cut like a knife. "Have you eaten yet?" she asked finally, desperate to change the subject.

"No. That's why I came over, to see if you wanted to go out for supper. There's a new Vietnamese restaurant open just down the block. Yvan and I went there last week. They make the tastiest spring rolls. Want to try it?"

"Sure." She had very little appetite, but anything was better than sitting alone in the apartment. She would just have to make sure Reyn wasn't the subject of conversation. As good as her control was, it could slip, and then Gabby would take over again, trying to make everything all right.

RETURNING TO SCHOOL was what Caitlin needed. Unfortunately she had barely a week in the classroom before the start of Christmas break.

Christmas had never been her favorite time of year. It always made her realize just how alone she was. This year it was worse. Far worse. Missing Reyn was a constant gnawing ache. She hadn't thought it possible to want someone so much. There wasn't a minute in the day when she didn't long to be with him. She wanted to watch him paint, to hear his voice, to have him admonish her for not eating enough. He'd become a necessary part of her life and now he was gone. She felt the gap. She hurt and she was lonely.

What was Reyn doing? she wondered, as she shut her classroom door on the last day of school before the holidays. Would he spend Christmas with his father and stepmother? Or had he made arrangements to spend the time with Stevie? Not that it really made that much difference. The only thing that really mattered was that he wouldn't be with her.

"Hey, Cait! Wait up." Gabby poked her head out of her classroom door. "I'll just be a sec." She popped back into her room and emerged a moment later, pulling on her jacket. "Holidays at last," she said, sighing happily. "Now if only I didn't have to spend most of it with Yvan's mother, instead of skiing in Banff like I'd hoped. Still, it beats working—I think," she added with a grimace as they began walking to the exit. "What about you? Did you get ahold of your mother?"

"Last night, finally. She's got plans, though. Her boyfriend is taking her to Las Vegas over the holidays. She's really looking forward to it." Nothing in Caitlin's voice showed her disappointment. But she'd hoped that just once her mother would have been there for her.

"And your dad?"

Caitlin shrugged. "He's got his own family. We really don't have much contact."

"So you're all alone over Christmas." Gabby frowned.

"Not really. I've got a few plans. Bet they beat your time with the Wicked Witch of the West," she added with a grin, wanting to change the subject.

Gabby groaned and rolled her eyes. "Anything would. If I didn't love Yvan so much, I wouldn't go near the woman." She held open the outer door while Caitlin unfurled her umbrella.

"At least by going to the Interior, you're likely to get out of the rain," Caitlin said, glancing up at the leaden sky.

"Yeah, and maybe see some snow. A white Christmas could make up for a lot." They stopped beside Gabby's car. "I don't like leaving, knowing you're going to be alone over Christmas, Cait. You could always come with us."

Caitlin raised her eyebrows in mock horror. "After your descriptions of Yvan's mother? Not on your life. Don't worry about me so much, Gabby. I'm okay. I've got plans. I won't be alone."

Gabby hesitated. "Are you sure?"

"Positive. Go on now. Have a Merry Christmas and don't let the old witch get you down."

"It'll take a lot more than her to ruin my Christmas," Gabby said, cheerful again. "By the way, did you hear from Reyn?"

Caitlin's heartbeat quickened as she shook her head. "I didn't really expect to." But that hadn't stopped her from wanting to. Just a simple Christmas card with his name scrawled across the bottom would have been welcome.

"Yeah, well, I thought he might have been in touch." She shrugged and grinned. "I guess there really *wasn't* anything brewing between the two of you.''

''I told you there wasn't,'' Caitlin said lightly, forcing a smile. ''Well, see you after the holidays.''

''If not sooner. I'll phone you when we get back, before we go over to Victoria to see my family. Have a Merry Christmas, Cait.'' She started the engine and drove off, turning to wave goodbye.

Caitlin shifted the pile of books in her arms and started slowly for home, dreading the holidays that loomed ahead.

CAITLIN FOUGHT HARD to keep depression from overwhelming her. She knew from past experience that when things got too much to bear, keeping busy was the best solution. She spent her days helping to wrap and deliver hampers of food and gifts for needy families throughout the city. Before night set in, she walked the paths that led around Stanley Park. The sight and smell of the ocean took her back to her time on the island with Reyn. It had been such a brief interlude, but it had meant everything to her. If only it could have been forever.

The holidays passed in a blur. Volunteer work might help Caitlin to keep her perspective, but still, the pain didn't stop. It was a relief to return to school.

Her class was always unsettled after the holidays. Most of her students came from troubled or broken homes, where Christmas was a time of heavy drinking, depression and increased domestic violence. And Caitlin found it heartbreaking to see how this affected the children.

Derek, a blond and freckled seven-year-old, seemed especially unhappy. He'd spent most of the first afternoon with a black crayon clutched in his grubby fist, slashing it across sheet after sheet of paper. When his anger became too much, he threw the crayon box at the little girl seated across from him, causing her to cry silent pitiful tears. Caitlin sent him to the "time out corner," where he sat wordlessly, his face mutinous, rocking back and forth in his chair.

Caitlin kept him after class. She pulled up a seat in front of him and looked at him seriously.

"Derek, you hurt Lonie when you threw those crayons at her. We don't hurt people here, no matter how angry we are. You know that, don't you?"

He gave a tight nod.

Caitlin reached over, pushing back a ragged strand of hair that fell across his pale face. "You're not very happy today," she stated quietly.

Derek stopped rocking and held his arms tight to his chest. "I'm real mad."

"At who, Derek?"

His shoulders heaved in a shrug and he expelled an angry breath.

"Did you see your dad at Christmas?" Caitlin asked, already knowing the answer.

"He *said* he'd come!" The words burst explosively from the little boy. "He promised! He was going to take me to a hockey game an' everything! I was going to go stay with him an' my new baby brother an'—an' everything!" Tears of fury and hurt spilled from the boy's eyes.

"Oh, Derek. I'm so sorry it didn't happen. I know how much you wanted to see your dad." This was far from the first time the father had broken his promise to the little boy. "How's your mom?"

Derek breathed in tremulously. "She's real sad. She cried all the time an' drank a lot of wine." He swiped at his tears, leaving a grimy streak across his cheek. "She said my dad didn't come 'cause I'm bad all the time," he added in a low voice.

"No, Derek," Caitlin said firmly. "It's not your fault your dad didn't keep his promise, and it's not your fault he left in the first place." She knew Derek had been led to believe his father's desertion was his fault.

"I try an' be good." The tears were flowing faster now.

Caitlin reached out and pulled him into her arms, feeling his tense little body relax against hers with a shuddering sob. "I know you do, Derek. I also know how angry and hurt you get sometimes. I sure would, too." She rocked back and forth a bit, patting him soothingly. She would get in touch with Derek's father—again—and let him know how much his broken promises hurt his son. She'd also try to convince the mother to seek help for her depression. Sometimes counseling could work wonders.

When Derek's sobs subsided, Caitlin fished a tissue from her pocket. "Wipe and blow," she commanded gently, smoothing his hair. "And then you'd better get yourself home before your mother wonders where you are. And remember, talk to me when you're mad, okay?"

Derek snuffled and nodded. "Okay."

Smiling, Caitlin stood up and pushed her chair back. As she turned around, her eyes widened in shock and a gasp of surprise escaped her lips.

Reyn was leaning against the doorjamb, arms folded. He stared at her with dark brooding eyes, his face set, the line between his brows cutting deep.

Caitlin turned quickly away, her heart bounding wildly. Why was he here? What did he want? If only she'd had some warning, some time to prepare, to steel herself against the tumult of emotions his unexpected presence caused.

With hands that trembled, she helped Derek into his jacket and zipped it up for him.

Subjugating her own feelings, she smiled down at Derek's upturned freckled face, wishing she could banish the pain and worry from his young life.

"I like you a lot, Derek Wilton," she said, stooping to give him a hug and a kiss.

"Even when I get mad an' be bad?" he asked, his voice still quavery.

"I like you all the time." She straightened the collar of his jacket. "Get yourself home now, sweetie. I'll see you tomorrow."

As Derek turned to leave, he noticed Reyn standing in the doorway. His eyes widened much as Caitlin's had, and he studied the man for a moment.

Reyn left the doorway and came into the room, his face softening as he smiled gently at the boy. "Hello."

Derek ducked his head, then looked up with a gap-toothed grin. "Hi, bye." He scampered from the room.

Caitlin went to stand behind her desk and nervously sorted some papers. Why didn't Reyn say something? Anything?

She glanced at him. He stood watching her, his arms still folded across his chest, his face locked once again into hard lines. His eyes were heavy-lidded and distant, but an undeniable anger sparked in their depths.

She forced herself to speak. "Hi," she said. Anything to break the cold silence. "Did you come to see Gabby?"

"Gabby doesn't know I'm here. It's you I want to talk to."

"Oh." Caitlin opened a desk drawer and pushed some papers into it. She swallowed nervously. "What about?"

"You should know." The words were forced from between tight lips.

She shook her head in agitation. "Reyn, I—"

"Not here," he interrupted, his tone brusque, impatient. "Your place."

"My place? But..." Her voice trailed off as she caught the look on his face. Maybe that would be best.

HANDS SHAKING with nervousness, Caitlin opened the door to her apartment and went inside. Reyn followed closely, shutting the door behind him with a loud thud.

The kitten trotted into the room. Caitlin picked her up, then perched on the edge of the armchair.

"Lily's grown a lot," she said in a small voice. *Something* had to be said to break the silence pulsing between them.

Reyn turned to her in irritation. "I didn't come here to talk about animals."

Caitlin took a deep breath and let it out slowly. His obvious anger upset her. "Then what?" she asked diffidently.

His gaze was stony. "You left without saying goodbye."

"I—I left a note."

He gave a derisive snort.

"What? Gotta go, it was nice knowing you, have a nice life?"

"It was more than that, Reyn," she protested.

"Not a hell of a lot."

He was right. It hadn't been. But what did he want from her now? "I'm sorry."

"Sorry!" He shook his head in exasperation. "You left without a word—like you couldn't get away fast enough."

She looked at her hands. What he said was true, but how could she explain the hopelessness she'd felt knowing he didn't return her love, the sense of panic that came from knowing that he would surely guess her feelings—and pity her. "I'm sorry," she repeated. What else could she say?

"Yeah, so I gathered." He turned abruptly and strode to the door. "I guess I was hoping for more than that," he muttered.

"Reyn, wait. Please don't go." She couldn't bear for him to leave in such anger.

He stopped, his hand on the doorknob. "Give me one good reason I should stay."

She lifted her hands in a gesture of helplessness. "I—we're friends, aren't we?"

"I thought we were," he said quietly. "I'm not so sure anymore." He twisted the knob and stepped into the hallway.

"Wait!" Caitlin jumped up and flew to the door. She couldn't let him leave, not like this! "Wait, Reyn. Please." Her voice rose in desperation.

He just stood there, his back to her. She saw his shoulders rise as he took a deep breath, felt him tense when she laid a hand on his arm. She removed it quickly. He turned and looked down at her, his face stony.

Her eyes were pleading and a little bit frightened. "I made a mistake, leaving like that. Please. Let's talk about it."

"Is there anything left to say?"

"I don't know. But you can't leave like this."

His lips curled in a bitter smile. "Can't I? At least *I* won't be sneaking away in the dead of the night."

She winced, hating the look on his face. "Reyn, come back inside."

He stared broodingly at her, then nodded abruptly. He moved back inside and went to sit on the couch.

Relieved, Caitlin shut the door, resting against it for a brief moment. She had to know why Reyn had come, why he was so angry with her. Taking a deep breath for strength, she turned to have things out with him.

"All right," she said determinedly. "Tell me what's wrong."

The anger was gone from his face, replaced by a cool remoteness. He stood up suddenly and went to the window, hands jammed into his pockets, looking out on the street below.

"Reyn?" she whispered, wanting him to speak. Surely nothing he had to say would be as bad as his silence—his eloquent condemning silence.

He expelled a harsh breath and turned to her, back lighted by the window, his face shadowed.

"We spent the night making love . . . and then you sneaked away while I was sleeping. Think about it, Caitlin. How would *you* feel if I had done that to you?"

His words hit her like a slap in the face. She stared at him, mouth open and eyes wide.

"Paints a different picture, doesn't it?" he said harshly.

"Oh, Reyn," she whispered, appalled, seeing her actions in a new light. "I—I didn't think—"

"You thought that because I'm a man it wouldn't affect me," he interrupted coldly. "Well, let me tell you, trite as it sounds, cut us and we bleed, Caitlin. Men hurt, too."

Caitlin rubbed her hands together in agitation. "I'm—" She stopped. Apologizing again would serve no purpose. She looked up at him, wishing she could see his face more clearly. Had he come here only to chastise her?

She went to the couch and sat down heavily. "What do you want from me?" she whispered, aching inside.

He raised his hands in a gesture of exasperation. He went to sit across from her and leaned forward, his arms resting on his knees. "An explanation, Caitlin," he said quietly. "Why did you leave like that?"

Caitlin rubbed her thumb back and forth across her knuckles, as her teeth gnawed her bottom lip. How could she tell him the truth without revealing what she really felt?

He was watching her, his face still. "You can be honest," he said stiffly. "Was our lovemaking disappointing for you? Did I . . . hurt you?"

Her mouth fell open in surprise and she shook her head quickly. "Oh, Reyn, no! It was wonderful." Pictures of their intimacy flooded her mind, and her cheeks flushed with color. She ducked her head shyly.

His lips twitched in a suggestion of a smile. "That's what I thought," he murmured. "Then what, Caitlin. Tell me."

There was nothing left but to tell him the truth. "I was afraid."

"Afraid?" he repeated, frowning. "Of me?"

"No, of course not. It's just . . ." Her voice trailed off and she looked up, her eyes wide and vulnerable. "That last night with you meant everything to me, Reyn."

He frowned slightly and shook his head. "But you still left."

"I—I thought it would make things easier for me." She took a deep breath and continued. "I knew we couldn't be just friends anymore, and I didn't want an affair."

"Why didn't you want an affair?" he asked softly.

"Affairs eventually end and I didn't think I could handle it, becoming just another friend, like Stevie . . ." She stopped, eyes downcast.

"Why did that bother you so much?"

It was as if he knew the truth but was still determined to hear her say it. "I'm in love with you,

Reyn." It no longer seemed important to keep that from him. "And I need all that being in love entails."

"Right down to that rose-covered cottage and the white picket fence?"

She raised her chin defiantly. "Yes," she said firmly.

"Good."

Startled, she looked at him. He was grinning crookedly, his eyes soft and velvety, the hated anger banished from their depths. He moved to sit beside her.

"That's exactly what being in love means to me, too, Caitlin. I want it all, complete with the cat and dog on the hearth and babies sleeping upstairs."

He picked up her hand and kissed it. "It's the last thing I expected to happen, but I've fallen in love with you. Will you marry me?"

Caitlin's eyes mirrored her disbelief. This was so far from the bleak future she'd imagined for herself over and over again during the past desolate weeks. He was in love with her? It couldn't be happening.

"Really?" she asked, her doubt plain.

His fingers tightened on hers. "Really."

All the pain and longing she'd harbored since she'd fled the island welled up in her. Tears filled her eyes and her breath caught on a sob.

Reyn looked at her in dismay. "What's wrong?"

Caitlin shook her head, helpless to stop the tears. "I missed you so much."

Reyn pulled her to him. As she nestled into his shoulder, he rubbed his face against her hair. "I missed you, too, sweetheart," he said, his voice shaky. "Caitlin, I never thought I could feel that bad, but when I woke up and found you gone, I thought my world had ended again." His arms tightened as though he'd never let her go.

Caitlin squeezed her eyelids tight, stopping the flow of tears. It was crazy to cry now. The man she loved was here, with her, holding her in his arms, confessing *his* love for *her*. She sighed tremulously and wiped her cheeks. Pushing herself back, she looked at Reyn.

He smiled and wiped an errant tear from her face. "All right now?"

"I think so." She let out a ragged breath. "I've been so miserable for so long," she confessed. "It's hard to believe this is real."

"It's real, sweetheart," he said gruffly. "And it's forever. It feels so right, loving you . . . being loved by you."

He curled a finger under her chin and raised her face until she was looking at him. His soft velvety eyes held hers as he lowered his head to touch her lips with a cherishing kiss.

"I love you, Caitlin." The words were a warm whisper of breath against her mouth before his arms tightened and he kissed her deeply, as though he never wanted to stop.

THEY LAY ON CAITLIN'S BED beneath a jumble of covers. The kitten had decided to join them and lay curled up and purring on Reyn's stomach. Caitlin's head rested on Reyn's chest while he idly wove strands of her hair between his fingers.

"So?"

"So what?" she asked sleepily, running her thumb across the raspy jut of his jaw. It was wonderful to be able to touch him freely, with all the love she felt for him.

"I asked you a question a while ago. You didn't answer. Will you marry me, Caitlin?"

Caitlin rolled over and stared at the ceiling. This was where the real world came in again. There was only one answer she wanted to give, but . . .

He propped himself on his elbow and stared down at her. A frown was slowly replacing his look of relaxation. "Caitlin?"

She caught her bottom lip between her teeth and looked at him. "I want to . . ." she said in a low voice.

"But?" he asked tightly.

She searched for the right words. "I love your place on the island—I don't think I've ever felt so much at home anywhere else, but . . . my life here is important to me, Reyn. The kids need me, and I need them." There, she had said it. Could he understand how important her work was to her?

His breath gushed out in an obvious sigh of relief. "And here I thought you had some deep dark secret that would prevent us from getting married," he teased. He smiled at the worried light in her eyes and kissed her softly.

"Do you think I could love you like I do and not know how committed you are to those children? I saw what you did for that little guy this afternoon, how much you cared. Don't think for a moment that I want you to give up your job."

"How will we work it?" she asked, her eyes shining with relief.

"Easy. We'll live in Vancouver while you're working, and on the island during holidays. Nothing to it.

We'll need a bigger place than this, but that shouldn't be a problem. We can start looking later today." He glanced at the clock on the bedside table. "Well, maybe tomorrow. Now, is that it?"

She smiled and nodded.

"Then, Caitlin, for the last time—I hope—will you please marry me?"

She snuggled against him, her skin warming where it touched his. She lay her head on his shoulder, her cheek brushing against the hair-roughened hardness of his chest. "Oh, yes!" she breathed.

Only this morning a lifetime of unhappiness had stretched before her. She'd felt as dark and dreary as the winter day, her spirits doused by unrequited love. And now Reyn lay beside her, declaring his desire to share his life with her. It seemed a dream, but she was in his arms, his breath stirring her hair. She raised her head and kissed him.

"You make me so happy, Reyn," she whispered, feeling tears of wonder sting her eyes. "I love you more than I can say."

He returned her kiss with fervor. "And I love you, Caitlin. Thank God you came into my life."

EPILOGUE

EARLY-MORNING RAYS of sunshine fell across the deck outside the bedroom. Warming air held the tang of sea and cedar and the raucous call of a distant gull.

Caitlin leaned against the railing and looked out at the ocean, still a misty early-morning blue. The cat stretched on the railing beside her, full grown now and haughtily ignoring the dog.

Caitlin breathed deeply, a smile of happiness playing on her lips in spite of the discomfort she was in. As she rubbed the nagging pain in her lower back, she heard Reyn come through the patio door to stand behind her. She rested against him, his hands protectively cupping her taut swollen belly.

"Feeling okay?" he asked, rubbing his chin across her hair.

"I feel wonderful, but..." She turned around. "I think it's time, Reyn." She saw the look of panic race across his face and grinned ruefully.

"How long has it been?" he demanded. "Why didn't you wake me? You should have stayed with Edie—this island's no damned place for someone about to give birth. It's going to take us forever to get off. Let's get going."

Caitlin put a hand on his arm, stopping his rush into the house. "There's no need to get into a frenzy.

Honest. We've got hours yet. I want you to—'' Her voice broke off on a gasp of pain and she held her arms tight against her stomach.

As the contraction ended, she forced a smile. ''That one came a lot sooner than it was supposed to. Reyn . . . maybe we don't have that much time.''

His face paled. ''That does it. I'm phoning Dr. Palmer. She can come out of retirement for *this*. Sweetheart, come on. Lie down while I call.''

Caitlin frowned and shook her head. ''There's no need to bother Dr. Palmer. We can catch the next ferry and be at the hospital in less than an hour. Please, Reyn. Let's just go.''

''Dammit,'' he muttered, putting an arm around her. ''I should have made you listen to me. If anything happens to you . . .''

''Nothing's going to happen, Reyn,'' Caitlin said firmly. ''I'm strong and healthy, and having a baby takes forever. The doctor wouldn't have let me stay here if he thought there was a problem. Get dressed and then we'll go.'' The last word ended on a moan as another wave of pain rippled through her.

''I think—'' She gasped and bit her bottom lip, then tried to smile to ease the look of total panic on Reyn's face. ''I think maybe you'd better call Dr. Palmer, after all.''

THE DOCTOR CLOSED THE DOOR behind her, leaving the three of them alone.

Reyn eased himself onto the bed, looking down at his daughter cocooned in a soft flannel blanket against her mother's side.

"You scared the hell out of me, Caitlin," he said, pushing the still-damp hair back from her brow. "Next time, you'll stay at Edie's a month—two months!—before you're due."

Caitlin uttered a sleepy groan of protest. "Next time! Only a man would say that at a moment like this. I may never let you near me again."

He smiled lazily and rubbed a finger over her bottom lip. "Oh, yeah?"

"Yeah." She smiled at the look of love in his eyes. "She's beautiful, isn't she, Reyn?"

"Absolutely gorgeous." He pulled back a corner of the blanket and touched a finger to the baby's tiny clenched fist. "Just like her mother," he added, as he traced the curve of the baby's face and stroked the cap of soft downy hair. "She's perfect."

Caitlin nodded contentedly. "She is, isn't she. What will we name her?"

"Amanda, like we thought. It suits her. And—"

"Claire, after your mother," Caitlin finished. "We'll have to phone everyone."

"I'll do that once we get you two to the hospital."

Caitlin shook her head and frowned. "I don't want to go, Reyn. I want to stay here—just you and me and Amanda. I don't want anyone else."

"Neither do I, sweetheart, but we should be sure everything is okay. I'll worry otherwise. But for the moment..." He moved until she could rest her head on his shoulder. The baby slept in the warm close space between them.

Reyn stroked Caitlin's face. "You've made me happier than I ever thought possible. This last year has been wonderful, and today made everything perfect. I love you so much."

Caitlin found his hand and squeezed it. Her life was full of love and bright with promise. "I love you, too, Reyn," she whispered. "More than ever." She sighed in soft contentment as she felt his lips brush against her forehead.

"You've made everything wonderful," she said sleepily. "I couldn't ask for anything more." Her eyes drifted shut.

Reyn's arms tightened carefully around his family. "Neither could I, Caitlin. Neither could I."

THIS JULY, HARLEQUIN OFFERS YOU THE PERFECT SUMMER READ!

Sunsational

**EMMA DARCY
EMMA GOLDRICK
PENNY JORDAN
CAROLE MORTIMER**

From top authors of Harlequin Presents comes HARLEQUIN SUNSATIONAL, a four-stories-in-one book with 768 pages of romantic reading.

Written by such prolific Harlequin authors as Emma Darcy, Emma Goldrick, Penny Jordan and Carole Mortimer, HARLEQUIN SUNSATIONAL is the perfect summer companion to take along to the beach, cottage, on your dream destination or just for reading at home in the warm sunshine!

Don't miss this unique reading opportunity.

Available wherever Harlequin books are sold.

FIRST CLASS

Coming soon
to an easy chair near you.

FIRST CLASS is Harlequin's armchair travel plan for the incurably romantic. You'll visit a different dreamy destination every month from January through December without ever packing a bag. No jet lag, no expensive air fares and *no* lost luggage. Just First Class Harlequin Romance reading, featuring exotic settings from Tasmania to Thailand, from Egypt to Australia, and more.

FIRST CLASS romantic excursions guaranteed! Start your world tour in January. Look for the special **FIRST CLASS** destination on selected Harlequin Romance titles—there's a new one every month.

NEXT DESTINATION:
FLORENCE, ITALY

 Harlequin Books

This August, don't miss an exclusive
two-in-one collection of earlier love stories

MAN
WITH A PAST

TRUE COLORS

by one of today's hottest
romance authors,

Jayne Ann Krentz

Now, two of Jayne Ann Krentz's most loved books are
available together in this special edition that new and
longtime fans will want to add to their bookshelves.

Let Jayne Ann Krentz capture your hearts with the love
stories, MAN WITH A PAST and TRUE COLORS.

And in October, watch for the second two-in-one
collection by Barbara Delinsky!

Available wherever Harlequin books are sold.

TWO-K

Back by Popular Demand

Janet Dailey
Americana

A romantic tour of America through fifty favorite Harlequin Presents® novels, each set in a different state researched by Janet and her husband, Bill. A journey of a lifetime in one cherished collection.

In June, don't miss the sultry states featured in:

Title # 9 - FLORIDA
　　　　　Southern Nights
　　#10 - GEORGIA
　　　　　Night of the Cotillion

Available wherever
Harlequin books are sold.